WATCH
TIME
FLY

WATCH TIME FLY

Stories by
LAURA FURMAN

THE VIKING PRESS   NEW YORK

First published in 1983 by The Viking Press
40 West 23rd Street, New York, N.Y. 10010
Published simultaneously in Canada by
Penguin Books Canada Limited

The author would like to thank the John Simon Guggenheim Memorial
Foundation for its generous support. Several of the stories in this collec-
tion were written with the help of a CAPS grant from the New York
State Council on the Arts, for which the author is grateful.

"Listening to Married Friends" appeared originally in *Mademoiselle*;
"Free and Clear," "Real Estate," "For Scale," "Sweethearts," "Buried
Treasure," "Nothing Like It," and, in different form, "The Kindness
of Strangers," in *The New Yorker*; "Watch Time Fly," in *Vanity Fair*;
and "Arlene," in *Vision*.

Library of Congress Cataloging in Publication Data
Furman, Laura.
    Watch time fly.
    I. Title.
PS3556.U745W3   1983   813'.54   83-47871
ISBN 0-670-75016-6

Printed in the United States of America
Set in CRT Caslon

For Frances Kiernan
and Wendy Weil

CONTENTS

WATCH TIME FLY

One December evening on her return from class, Anna found a postcard from Warren in her mailbox. She pressed the button for the elevator and examined the picture on the card: it was of an orange magnified so many times the skin looked like the surface of a warm and glossy planet, the opposite of the violet winter outside. Until the elevator came, Anna listened to the all-news radio station her landlady played day and night to keep burglars away, then she tucked the postcard in her shoulder bag, went into the elevator, and used the slow trip to the fourth floor to study the walls for new drawings and mottoes.

Anna tried not to expect very much. She had established a routine and she followed it: secretarial work at a midtown tax accounting firm, dance class up the street from the office three evenings a week, a graduate class in social work to see if that might be her career. But Anna couldn't help imagining her life as an egg that was cracking very slowly—sooner or later a creature would emerge from the shell. The coming change was now only an inner conviction, a shape observed too closely to be discerned.

She had moved to the neighborhood less than a year before, and by moving downtown, Anna felt that she'd changed countries. On her walk home from the subway each night she checked the new landmarks: a Korean discount store that hung its wares from the canopy in all weather; a stone church that resembled a chess piece; the small corner store where she bought milk or juice in small containers from the nearly blind owner. He was afraid, he confided often in Anna, that an uptown gourmet takeout chain would try to take over now that he was old.

She was lucky to have found the apartment, she knew, and at first it seemed like a perfect place. Even the two little boys who lived next door with their mother, who was divorced, seemed proof of Anna's new brand of domesticity; in the Riverside Drive building where she'd lived with Warren there were few children. But afternoons and evenings the boys played a game of their own invention and until they went to sleep Anna had to listen to the thud of a ball hitting the apartments' common wall, the thunder of the chase.

Soon after she'd moved in Anna went next door and talked to their small, sharp-faced mother, whose black eyes sparked for a fight and who had introduced herself to Anna as Mrs. Morgan, not offering a first name, only a title.

Anna said, "I hate to complain, but the noise the boys make playing ball—"

She spoke softly and made self-deprecating gestures to downplay the intent of her speech—a request that they stop the game forever. She was surprised when Mrs. Morgan exploded at her. Everything was wrong, it seemed: the way Anna left her umbrella outside her door and let a stream of water trickle to Mrs. Morgan's welcome mat on rainy days; the noise late at night, after the eleven o'clock news, of Chopin on Anna's stereo; that Anna's phone had rung once thirty times on a night when Anna was out of town.

In a flash of intuition, Anna guessed that Mrs. Morgan would have liked to invoke the authority of the absent Mr. Morgan, as Anna would have liked to call up a masculine party to settle the matter. But there were only the two women in the hallway and the little boys caged in their room, thumping the ball even then. Anna backed away from the small furious woman and retreated into her apartment, locking the door behind her.

"Boys playing," she heard echoing in the tile hallway. "In this day and age you complain about boys playing!"

Anna made a wish that Mrs. Morgan would soon marry a wealthy man and move elsewhere. If not, she thought, the boys would grow up and leave home, but what would become of Anna? Was she to remain silent through their childhood years of wall basketball and their adolescent wild music? Who had called her and rung thirty times and never bothered to call again?

The bright orange postcard was bent when she left the elevator, hunted for her keys in her crowded shoulder bag, opened the door to her apartment. Anna put everything on the floor and locked the door behind her, then turned on the lights and examined the card. Warren had settled in Los Angeles. When they'd separated legally, he'd tried staying in New York in their apartment. Then he'd bought a van, equipped it with tapes and coolers full of New York food and drink, and he'd set off across country. "I'm going to forget you," Warren told Anna in their last phone call and she'd replied, "Fine," wondering if he could.

In L.A., she read, *great town. Not New York. Living with Susan. We may open shop here. Me a shopkeeper? In New York soon. Love to you, W.*

Anna set the postcard on her mantel. The fireplace didn't work and she'd filled it with a jug of heavy-scented dust-catching eucalyptus. She pulled the drapes shut and turned on more lights against the gloom. Her apartment was on a side street a few blocks north of the Village, her living-room windows facing a warehouse, her kitchen and bedroom overlooking an alley. She'd never bought furniture before nor made any decisions about decorating. Warren had been very good at it, and if he bought something he didn't like—"Doesn't work," he'd say without regret—he'd give it to the Salvation Army.

She needed more color in the room, Anna decided. She dressed in primary colors, showing up for work in pressed straight-leg blue jeans, bright red or blue crew-neck sweaters ("Like a boy!" said one of the secretaries, "with that Peter Parsky haircut!"), but she hadn't dared to use color in the apartment. In the spring, if she had the money, she'd buy a red rug and lay it between the fireplace and the sofa. She wouldn't see Warren and Susan if they came to New York. The divorce would be official in April and it would happen very smoothly, the lawyer promised. What good would it do her to see Warren, except to stir her up in some way she couldn't imagine, causing feelings she didn't want to have.

It had first occurred to Anna that she needn't stay married to Warren on an autumn night the year before, a night when they were supposed to be feasting on homemade noodles and fresh tomato sauce. They'd planned to spend the afternoon cooking the sauce from fourteen pounds of Florida tomatoes Anna had bought at a fruit stand on Broadway. Warren was worrying about money, as he did periodically, and he'd decided it would quell his anxiety to see jars of sauce displayed in the kitchen. But the sauce had burned while Anna was on the phone, and the noodle dough crumbled in Warren's hands.

Unaccountably, Warren cheered up and said, "Let's eat out." He wanted to get dressed up and eat in a fancy restaurant. Anna wanted to skip dinner and go to sleep. The waste exhausted her and the sudden change of mood. Her arms still ached from carrying the tomatoes. They compromised—neither wanted a fight—by going to a modest French restaurant off Broadway in the Sixties.

Warren ordered snails, which Anna loved but tackled only when she felt capable of handling both the tight metal clamp and the possibility of a round greasy shell skidding across the table.

"It's hard to believe how many of those tomatoes were rotten," Warren said. "Did you look at them before you bought them?"

"The top layer," Anna said. "What did you want me to do—lay them all out on Broadway?"

"Sometimes I think people see you coming, Anna.

They get out their questionable goods then and there.
Here's a live one, they say. Here's one for the books."
She spoke the thought as soon as it came to mind.
"How about it," Anna said. "What if we just call it a
day?"

She observed him closely as she spoke, his thick eyebrows, his light curls that rested like a halo around his
delicate, bony face. Butter from the snails made his rose-
bud mouth glow.

"You're kidding," he said.

"No," she said. "Think it over."

When they were first married, Anna was charmed by
the number of things Warren couldn't do for himself.
She felt obliged to take on herself the simple tasks that
dismayed him. He was stunned by small tediums and she
was almost grateful that it was so, for here was a way she
could demonstrate that she loved him and was essential to
him. She would not have imagined in the early days that
this feeling was based on the fact that Warren was rich
and she penniless.

They'd met in boarding school, where Anna was on
full scholarship. The differences in their homes seemed
an indication, willy-nilly, that they were meant for each
other and destined to create together a beautiful alternative. Even as a teenager, Warren knew how to dress and
what food to order in restaurants. He knew all the new
films and painters, rock groups and styles long before
anyone else. For years Anna had no idea what he saw in
her. They married in college and Warren dropped out
without finishing his degree. Anna nearly had a Master's

when she dropped out, landing comfortably on Warren's routine, living each day as it came, with no larger questions in mind than where they would travel in Europe each spring, where they might live if ever New York tired them.

Anna smoothed his daily path as she had while she was a student. But living on Warren's largesse, with no occupation but his comfort, Anna caught herself adding up the minutes and hours it took to run a simple household for two: cleaning, cooking, caring for wardrobes, answering mail, paying bills and keeping track of his obligations, apologizing when he stood someone up, begging off when he didn't want to honor an obligation. She anticipated difficulties for Warren and protected him from worry.

Now, at the thought of not doing anything for Warren ever again, Anna felt endowed with a hearty appetite for her pâté and crusty bread, with a sudden affection for the brightly colored stylized maps of the French provinces that decorated the restaurant.

They had been together so long, Anna thought. Soon she would be thirty. Warren would always be with her, so why need he stay there at all?

On an unexpectedly bright morning in March, Warren called Anna at the office. The machines were clattering and phones ringing. Tax season was in full swing. "Now we all pay!" was the office motto.

"I haven't heard your voice in so long," Warren said.

"How long has it been? Susan and I were trying to figure it out on the plane. She thinks it's been since April. At the lawyer's. I wasn't sure."

"Less than a dozen months," Anna said. He'd called her in September on her birthday. She wouldn't remind him of that. And maybe it was he who'd called in the middle of the night and let it ring thirty times. She wouldn't ask. "How did you like the sweater I sent for Christmas? It was a great color for you. I figured it might get cold out there once in a while."

"Didn't I thank you? Didn't I write?" Warren sounded stricken. "I was sure I had."

"Never mind," Anna said.

"It's funny. I'm staying in our old neighborhood," Warren said. "Some cousin of Susan's has a townhouse on Seventy-seventh between Riverside and West End. He went to Bermuda and left us the place."

"Nice of him. You land on your feet, don't you?"

"I like the way he's done the house," Warren said, his voice growing momentarily faint, as if he were surveying a large room. "You'll have to come see it. As a matter of fact . . ."

Apologizing for the short notice, Warren invited Anna to come uptown that night for dinner. Susan wouldn't be able to join them—she was seeing an old friend—but she wanted to meet Anna. Warren gave Anna the address and as she copied it down Anna wondered why he wanted to see her, why Susan wanted to meet her. Perhaps there was nothing left for Warren, not even anger—he sounded so distant and friendly on the phone. But in any case, why propose dinner? She told him she'd be there around seven.

Anna had a hard time in class. She didn't follow combinations and her body was uncooperative. Her turnout was sloppy, her head was bent unbecomingly. The high-pitched voice of her teacher, a former Broadway dancer, shouted corrections but it seemed to come from far away. Anna was distracted but she suspected it was more a problem of her body than her mind. As a child, she'd been quite a ballerina. She'd been good enough, at least, so that her teacher allowed her to join the adult classes one night a week. Because of her superior elevation, Anna was often chosen to demonstrate leaps and fancy combinations. She covered the floor easily. After class, in the dressing room, she was uncomfortable with the adults. It was not only the difference in their bodies—her child's smoothness, their adult curves, their flesh let loose from the disciplining leotards—it was an attitude the older women had toward Anna. They doubted her, though she could leap all right and turn more times than they in a pirouette.

Anna looked out of the window, down onto Madison Avenue and Sixty-second Street. People were in a hurry. Soon she would be one of them, rushing across town. She looked at herself in the mirror and tried to focus her energy so that nothing would exist but her leap, her spotting, her turns—all less spectacular now that she was grown up. Concentration was her goal, not beauty. And the truth was, she saw, her leg aching from a slow stretch at the barre, she had only been young then, not especially good. She had been able to leap and turn because she was a child and had a child's flexibility and energy, the child's ignorance of the body's refusal to perform. Anna looked at the clock on the wall of the studio. Ten more minutes of this terrible adult knowledge and she would be on her way to Warren.

The temperature was dropping as she walked down Seventy-seventh Street toward the river. When the marriage was breaking up, Anna had been determined to move from this neighborhood, to abandon the broad changing river she could see from their pale blue bedroom, to leave behind the Broadway bazaar of fruit stands, butcher shops, specialty ice cream parlors. She didn't have much to move. All the good furniture was Warren's and Anna could have no objections. She accepted only a small settlement and would get no alimony. She felt more honest that way but she wondered if all along Warren had thought of the furniture and the money as his alone.

Some of the brownstones Anna passed had new façades of clapboard or wood shingles, modern windows, and steel gates, giving the block a raucous, uneven look. Susan's cousin had left his clumsy brownstone alone. In the bay window of the front parlor, filmy white lace curtains hung that might have belonged to the house when it was new.

The brownstone had entrances through the kitchen door a few steps below street level and up a broad set of steps that reached the parlor. Anna climbed the steps, choosing the more formal entrance. She rang the bell and waited.

The door was answered by a young woman with long fuzzy blond hair. She looked a little like Warren but was larger than he, with bright green eyes. She was pretty and unearthly looking.

"Hello," Anna said. "Susan?"

"I've heard so much about you," Susan said. "And I recognize you from the pictures."

"What pictures?" Anna asked.

Warren appeared at the door and he put his arm across Susan's shoulders. They wore matching sea-green cashmere sweaters.

"You remember," Warren said. "The ones we took in New Hampshire last spring."

He and Susan stood blocking the doorway, and it looked to Anna like an end to an evening rather than a beginning. Susan broke away, looking at her wristwatch and saying, "I'm going to be late as it is." She smiled quickly at Anna and went into the house, up a flight of dark wood stairs. Warren stepped aside to let Anna in.

He took Anna's coat and laid it on the seat of an elaborate hall tree on which a collection of hats—a boater, a canvas golf cap, a beat-up fedora—and canes were hanging.

"Let's go downstairs," Warren said. He led Anna through the narrow entryway, past a dimly lit Victorian parlor with heavy furnishings and the white curtains she'd noticed from the street, down a flight of stairs. "The kitchen is the best room in the house," he said.

It was a large modern room, gloss white with black cabinets. A round black Formica table with chrome legs took up the center of the room; on it was a pile of photographs, jewelry, and small leather-bound books. Red chairs were placed neatly around the table.

Susan came down the stairs soon after them, a tweed-lined raincoat over her arm.

"Warren," she said. "All I have is two twenties. Change? Do you have any change?"

While Warren searched his pockets and reassured Susan that he did have his keys, Anna sat at the table and looked at the photographs. She recognized the smiling people, friends she'd shared with Warren, whom she hadn't seen in months. A year before in March, Warren and Anna had visited them at a farm in New Hampshire that they were renting and were considering buying. Warren and Anna had been invited up to help tap maple trees but they'd gotten too involved in cooking—Warren had brought along a new food processor, one with many attachments—to tap more than the one tree featured in the photos. Anna and Warren wore matching lumber jackets, and Anna wondered what had become of hers. She was laughing hard in many of the photos, her mouth open in a way that was unflattering. She was annoyed that Susan had been looking at the photos. On the long drive back to New York from New Hampshire, Anna and Warren had decided to see a lawyer and to start divorce proceedings.

Anna turned to look over at Warren and Susan, who were still handing money back and forth. Susan looked fragile but her voice was businesslike. She was tanned in a permanent way, the tan of someone who lived year round in the sun, unlike a hard-earned Eastern tan, Anna decided.

"We'll see you again while we're in New York," Susan said to Anna. "I'd love to come to dance class with you. Warren says you're very good."

"I'm not," Anna said. "Never was, never will be."

"Well, I really want to spend some time with you while I'm East. I think it's important."

"Fine," Anna said, thinking that Susan would never call. "Warren has my phone number."

Susan kissed Warren and rubbed his back between the shoulder blades, then she left. Warren and Anna listened to her footsteps on the stairs, the opening and closing of the front door.

Warren smiled in a lazy, contented way. "Let's have some wine," he said. "I have a great zinfandel here. At least it should be great. How would you like to see *Rebel Without a Cause* after dinner? It's at the New Yorker."

"Doesn't it play in Los Angeles?"

It seemed odd to Anna to be on the verge of divorce and to see an old favorite movie with Warren. *Rebel Without a Cause* struck her as the kind of movie that would play often in L.A., but Anna knew nothing about California and conceived of it in emblems, like those on a slot machine—palms, convertibles, lemons.

"I haven't seen it for months. Honestly. At least, not since I left New York, I think. I lose track," Warren said. He handed Anna a heavy cut-glass goblet of red wine and sat across the table from her.

"You'd like it in California," Warren said. "We live on the edge of a Mexican neighborhood in an old bungalow. We just painted it hot pink with yellow trim. Canary yellow. I'm thinking I might go back to school. UCLA."

"What would you study?" Anna asked, thinking, A pink house?

"Education," Warren said. "Or anthropology. I might want to teach. I don't know. And in the meantime, Susan's really hot about this shop. She wants to open it to sell fresh flowers and posters, crafts that people in the neighborhood do. Hand-painted stationery. Pots."

"Junk," said Anna, trying to make her opinion sound friendly.

"In some people's terms," Warren said evenly.

"It sounds like a full life," Anna said. "Really. I mean it. It sounds as though you've changed."

"Well," Warren said. "As much as people change." He pushed the photos to one side and picked up the jewelry piece by piece. "Isn't this wild? We got bored last night and started looking through the drawers in the bedroom dresser. The guy's not married but he's got all these gewgaws. Maybe he has a girlfriend."

"And the little books?"

"Diaries. Pretty day-to-day, ordinary stuff, all in all. But look at this."

Warren held up a tiny watch, an oval gold pendant suspended from an elaborate gold bow that was studded with diamonds.

"It's from some fancy French jeweller," Warren said. "Susan says it might have been her aunt's. She isn't sure.

She's thinking of asking her cousin to give it to her but she doesn't know him very well."

"How would she explain the fact that she found it while you were going through his drawers?" Anna asked.

Warren drained his glass and refilled it, adding some to Anna's.

"Susan can do it," he said. "She thinks of ways to get what she wants."

The phone rang, and while Warren was talking, touching his pants pockets, reaching for a jacket that lay on the kitchen counter and patting it also, Anna looked at the watch, which was smaller than her thumb. It made her feel enormous even to hold it. It might have been created for a very small woman or a large doll, she thought, putting it back on the table beside the photos and the other pieces of jewelry.

"That was Susan," Warren said, hanging up.

"Something wrong?"

"No," he said. "Just calling." He reached for the goblet and drained the wine quickly. "We'd better get along if we're going to make the last show."

"O.K.," Anna said. She felt saddened, certain that he wanted to go to the movies to avoid talking to her. "Where shall we eat?"

"I thought," Warren said, looking at Anna from under his soft eyebrows, "let's eat at the Rendezvous. We used to like it. Or there's a new pasta place."

"The Rendezvous is fine with me," Anna said. It was on the way to the movie. "I don't care." She stood and put her bag over her shoulder.

"Wait," Warren said.

"What is it?" She remembered, annoyed, that Warren always found a reason to stay, as if he couldn't bear to go out a door when he was supposed to. "Lose your keys?"

"Very funny," he said, and made the same patting gestures to his pants pockets as he'd made while on the phone with Susan. "I have them right here. No, I want you to have the pictures."

"These?" She looked down at the pile on the table and back at Warren. "But I don't want them, Warren."

"Oh, come on. I brought them all the way from L.A. for you."

"Don't you want them?" Anna asked.

"I have the negatives," he said.

"No," Anna said. "It was a nice gesture, but no, I don't think so."

"Come on," Warren said. "Here. Fifty-fifty," and he scooped up the greater part of the pile and put the photos into Anna's big bag, which held her dance shoes and leotards, her wallet and makeup.

"They'll get crushed in there," she said, and considered putting them back on the table. Warren looked pleased with himself, as if he'd accomplished something by getting her to take the photos.

"We'd better go," he said gently, as if Anna had been stalling. "It would ruin my dinner if I thought we'd be late for the movie."

In the movie theatre, Anna turned away from the screen and looked at Warren. His shadowed pretty face seemed of a vintage with the trio of actors in the movie, those old adolescents. Would Warren grow old faster in California?

Dinner had been easy. The restaurant had been repainted since they were last there, but the chicken paprikash was the same. Warren had asked about her ballet lessons and her apartment. He said, "I didn't think I'd get through the first month without you," but it got better more quickly than he would have imagined. "I worried about you," he said, to Anna's surprise. "I thought about all those rotten tomatoes and I wondered how you'd get along without me."

The movie would finish and they would say goodbye. Perhaps when Warren was in New York again he would call. Or once the divorce was final (four weeks now, not very far away) he might not think of her. She would never go to Los Angeles. She would not call him. They would forget each other, Anna thought.

Warren turned and smiled at Anna. He tilted his head toward her and kissed her on the cheekbone, the corner of her eye, then took her hand. Warren settled back to watch the movie, his face relaxing into a sterner mask.

His skin smelled the same, Anna thought, a child's fresh pink smell.

After they'd eaten in the French restaurant and she had decided that they should part, they'd taken a cab along the broad Hudson, up Riverside Drive. When they reached home, they went to bed. There were fresh sheets on the bed, a set that matched the blue walls of their bedroom. Anna had stood naked at the window, looking out over the river and the black night sky, the taste of good food and wine still sweet in her mouth. Warren had come up beside her and they'd embraced, then made love with a concentration and passion that moved her. Was it possible to have a pleasant farewell, she'd wondered, and would it be farewell after all. While Warren slept, Anna stayed up late as she could, reading by the light of her small bedside lamp, unwilling to let the night pass. She thought of the future, when she might be alone in a place she hadn't yet seen.

Warren turned again to Anna in the half-light of the movie. He took his hand from hers and rubbed his wrist.

"You're supposed to be looking at the silver screen, sugar," he said. He moved in his seat, then reached once more for Anna's hand.

At the end of the movie Anna looked over at Warren again. He was transfixed by the tears being shed on the screen, but, Anna thought, he'd always had the enviable ability to forget everything around him, and she'd made it easy for him to be that way. In exchange for his forgetfulness, she got his company and his privileges. Anna remembered sharply her anguish and her relief the first weeks of separation when she realized she had only to keep track of herself.

Outside the movie theatre, Warren seemed subdued.

"I can't take it when the kid dies," Warren said, "no matter how many times I see it." He stood at the curb and raised his hand to flag down a cab. When one came, Warren ushered Anna into it. Once she was seated, Warren leaned into the cab, his hand on the roof.

"I've been burning it at both ends," Warren said.

"I'm going to stroll back. I promised Susan I'd be there. She doesn't like being alone. She's afraid of New York."

"I understand," Anna said. "I have to be at work any-way early in the morning," though she'd assumed they would go for coffee or a drink after the movie.

"I'll call," Warren said. "You have our number."

He put his hand to his mouth, then touched Anna's forehead. He slammed the cab door shut and Anna gave the driver her address.

She put on a kettle of water for tea and looked out the window to the dark alley below. She heard a rustling noise, then the cry of cats fighting or flirting.

Eavesdropping on cats, she thought, burning it at nei-ther end.

She turned off the kettle and slowly got ready for bed.

Anna stood impatiently in the long Friday bank line, waiting to deposit her paycheck, worrying that she'd be late for class. She reached into her shoulder bag for some lip gloss and found, among the photos and credit cards that had spilled from her wallet, the little watch. Her lip gloss had opened and encrusted the diamond bow, coated the crystal. Anna wiped it with a Kleenex and looked at the back of the watch, barely able to make out the tiny engraving of a French name and an address in Paris. Could I pawn it, she wondered, and knew she would do the right thing and return it to Warren and Susan. She hadn't planned to see them again nor did she believe they wanted to see her. She had composed a short excuse— now useless—that she thought she'd recite if they called her again.

At ten o'clock, Sunday morning, a hushed domestic hour on the side street, Anna stood at the parlor door of the townhouse. She pressed the bell and heard a distant trill. She waited and pressed the bell again. Anna couldn't be sure if she'd heard a noise inside the narrow house. If you were in an upstairs bedroom, Anna thought, lying in a state between sleeping and dreaming, perhaps the bell would be part of the morning noise, nothing to rouse you. She pressed the bell again and waited.

No one came, but Anna was now sure they were inside. A bell sounded different inside an empty house. She pressed the bell again. She would give it up, Anna thought, and she would go back downtown. She glanced over at the bay window of the Victorian parlor. The white curtain was moving. A hand pulled away from it. A blond head disappeared from view. It was all so fast, Anna couldn't be sure if it was Susan or Warren. Whichever, now that they knew who was ringing, they'd come to the door.

When long minutes had passed and no one came, no sound was heard, Anna thought of dropping the watch through the mail slot. But she left with the watch in her bag. She walked down the front stoop and up the block toward Broadway.

Sunday was a slow day, Anna thought, though worse in the anticipation. She would buy a *Times* on the way home and some sweet rolls from the bakery on Broadway and Seventy-ninth. She would read the paper, then study. In the evening, she'd find a friend to go with her to Chinatown to a noodle shop she'd heard about. As she walked up the street, Anna recalled the feel of the smooth blue sheets and of Warren's soft skin against her mouth, the sound of the river at their bedroom window.

Warren called at the end of the week, just as Anna was leaving work for an afternoon class.

"The visit's almost over," Warren said. "It just slipped past us. We're leaving day after tomorrow. I thought we'd see much more of you, Anna, but . . . Susan really wanted to get to know you."

"I can't imagine why," Anna said. "Maybe when the divorce is final we'll all join hands and celebrate. Is that what she has in mind?"

"That's just a formality," Warren said. "It is to me. We had what we had, and now . . . By the way. Have you seen that watch?"

"Watch?"

"The one I had—Susan's cousin's watch. I can't find it."

"Did you try your pockets?" Anna suggested. "Maybe it fell underneath the table."

"We've looked everywhere," Warren said. "All the

obvious places. Are you sure you don't remember if I did something with it?"

"You showed it to me. I remember it."

"But after that?"

"It's just a watch," Anna said. "Offer to buy him another one."

"Oh, come on," Warren said. "I haven't even met the guy and now I have to tell him this watch is missing. From a dresser drawer. Great."

"I have to get off the phone," Anna said. "It's tax time. We all pay."

"O.K.," Warren said. "O.K. We'll talk again before we go, I promise. Maybe we can all meet for a drink. Or lunch. Lunch tomorrow? I can't commit—I don't know if Susan has anything planned. I could call again."

"Maybe," Anna said. "Maybe. I have to go now."

That evening after class Anna got off the subway one stop ahead and she walked home. Her hair was still damp from her exertions and the air felt cold against her skull. She stopped at the church that looked like a chess piece and inspected the derelict winter garden, the marble statue of Jesus with his hands extended, palms up to the darkening sky.

Anna wished it were years ahead, a day when she would walk down the street and not recognize Warren if she passed him. They had gotten what they wanted from her: Susan took a good look and saw that Warren wasn't attached anymore; Warren saw he hadn't missed anything by leaving. She didn't mind that she'd lost Warren as a friend. There were other people in the world who would be her friends. Anna didn't mind the possibility that she had been wrong to send Warren away from her, nor did she mind very much the knowledge that they might have coasted along as they were for years without too much pain for her. But Anna resented the curtain being closed against her, her presence on the stoop ignored as if she were an eager petitioner for their company, a Fuller Brush man or a Jehovah's Witness.

When she reached her street, Anna felt too tired and chilled to stop at the corner store for the next morning's orange juice. The news blasted from the radio as she passed her landlady's door, and her own apartment greeted her with the steady sounds of basketball next door. Anna walked to her kitchen, flipped on the overhead fluorescent light, which flickered in a threatening way. She opened the kitchen window and let the cold outside air mingle with the stale heated air of the apartment.

There was no one in the alley below. Anna leaned out and saw bulging sacks of garbage, bent trash cans, and mangled tops fallen at precarious angles. She reached over to the kitchen counter and found the watch. She touched the cool diamond bow. The watch was silent. Anna held it to her ear and heard faint expensive whirrings, and as she listened to the perfect rhythms, Anna leaned out the window once again. The watch disappeared almost as soon as Anna opened her hand. She looked down into the dark alley and saw nothing. She listened and heard nothing. She thought: Why did the moron throw the clock out the window?

Warren called her at home two days later to say that he and Susan expected the cousin home any minute. They were leaving later; they'd have lunch with him, then go to the airport.

"I told Susan what you said, but she insisted on going to the Rendezvous and the movie theatre. And we've been through my coat pockets and jacket pockets. Susan wanted me to ask you again. Just to be sure."

He sounded annoyed but Anna couldn't tell if it was because Susan obviously didn't believe her and had put Warren up to calling, or if Warren didn't believe Anna either. Had he defended her to Susan, Anna wondered.

"You still have time to buy him something else before he arrives, don't you?" Anna suggested.

"It's a question of the embarrassment," Warren said. "This is putting me in a very awkward position."

Anna imagined the tense expression on Warren's face, the cigarettes he was lighting and stabbing out in the presence of a crisis. Susan would be scrambling in an irritated, hurried way, as Anna had scrambled so many times to help Warren.

Even then, when Anna had gone so far, she was tempted to save Warren by saying, "I know where the watch is, sugar." Instead Anna said, "What a shame. On your last day, too."

"It's been a great visit otherwise," Warren said.

"Things that are missing always turn up," Anna said.

"One way or another." She waited for him to say something, hoping Warren would find a way to end the conversation.

"Have a good flight," she said, and when he was still silent, she spoke again. "I hope you're happy out there."

At last, Anna said, "Goodbye."

LISTENING *to* TO MARRIED FRIENDS

F ifty feet ahead of Arla's car, a black cat crossed the Taconic Parkway. Arla sped up, hoping to see some saving white on its paws or neck, but she was too late. The cat disappeared into the woods along the road, and she was left with the conviction that it was a completely black cat. She waited for a consequence and, miles on, saw a white bird in the road. It looked like a seabird, though the ocean was hundreds of miles away. The bird sat on the pathway between her tires, and Arla thought that if she went very fast, she could pass over before the bird even noticed her approaching. She heard the flutter of wings, the sound of the car striking the bird. When she looked through the rearview mirror, she saw a gray spot, lighter than the color of the asphalt road. She had killed the bird. It wasn't deliberate, she told herself. It was the black cat's fault. Still, she worried the rest of the ride to Carl and Harriet's. She would tell them about the cat and the bird, though she didn't know how they felt about omens.

They had met when the couple lived in New York. Since their move upstate, Arla had visited them once or twice a year. Carl came to the city three days a week. One day, several weeks before, Arla had bumped into him on Madison Avenue, two blocks from the gallery he owned. They'd eaten at a luncheonette nearby and Carl had invited her for this weekend. The three had been closest when Carl and Harriet were deciding whether to leave New York and move to the country. Arla could have told them they would go; she could recognize the symptoms in her friends. Normal complaints about the air, the subway, and the rudeness of humanity escalated and became personal grievances; the apartments her friends lived in were spoken of as the apotheosis of the New York apartment. Having reached the top and found it unsatisfactory, they left the city—in Carl and Harriet's case for Columbia County.

Around the time Carl and Harriet were looking for a country house, Arla grew restless also and decided that she needed more space. As it was, she lived in the Village. Her studio took up the largest room, she had no guest room, and her kitchen was the size of a normal closet. She had considered taking their apartment on Riverside Drive, and Carl and Harriet thought of keeping hers for Carl to stay in when he worked in the city. All their common friends told Arla that Harriet and Carl's apartment was too big for one person. It was true that the rent would have been high for her alone, but she would have enjoyed the room. She'd formulated that each person takes up the same amount of space at one time, married or single. In the end, Carl had settled for a place around the corner from his gallery. He didn't want to live downtown again, he said; that was part of his past. He'd lived with a man, Arla remembered hearing, and it had ended badly.

And Arla decided that she had lived downtown too long to leave. The Upper West Side looked too lonely to her, too much sky by the river, too many giant buildings on the broad avenues. The feeling that claiming such a big space for herself alone would keep her alone was a small part of her decision. In the Village, she kept the hope of meeting the right person as she walked along a small street; meanwhile, she liked looking in windows and seeing rooms she admired, even if she would never enter them.

Arla wanted to be making the last miles to Carl and Harriet's with someone at her side. She wished when she arrived to be given the bedroom with the large bed instead of the one with the better view of the river, the prettier quilt, and the single bed. She was tired, her eyes were tired. She had sat too long finishing the pen-and-ink drawings for a book of fairy tales; there had been one moral to illustrate for each of the ten tales. Now as she drove she told herself not to look for the lump in the mattress. It was a sunny day in June and she was on her way to the country. She remembered, though, that Carl and Harriet had met when Harriet applied for a job in Carl's gallery. Arla had never met a man through work, she thought, but perhaps you had to be willing to sit in an office in order to meet someone, and she worked free-lance. She traced the stories of her friends' marriages and affairs and compared them with her own stage in life and her state of mind. She would have liked to discover through congruence that in one or two weeks her solitude would end. She was as used to her life as her married friends were to theirs, and she had made as many adjustments to herself as they ever had to each other. Arla wondered who could be wonderful enough that she would wish to rearrange her life, and then she thought, I'm an old maid. I'm getting crotchety.

Harriet was kneeling on the front lawn when Arla drove up. Harriet looked up and waved but she didn't stand. Arla left her car and walked across the lawn to her friend. Her legs felt springy after three hours in the car. She bent, kissed Harriet, and asked, "What are you doing?"

"It's time to put the tulips to sleep," Harriet said. "I'm sick of it. I could let them stay in the ground all year. Everybody else does. Why should I have to dig them up, pack them away in sawdust—which I haven't gotten yet from the lumberyard *twelve* miles away—when I only have to replant them again in a few months?"

"You've convinced me," Arla said. "Why indeed?" She thought Harriet might be kidding but there was a querulous tone to her voice.

"Don't laugh," Harriet said. "Carl's convinced the tulips will blow their color. He insists. But the hell with the tulips. You've cut your hair, I see."

When Harriet stood up, Arla had to remind herself that it wasn't Harriet's fault that she was so much taller than Arla nor that she had the clear, pleasing features of a child. There was a six-inch difference between the women, and Arla felt short and fat around Harriet. Harriet had always been thin. She never did sit-ups morning and night to keep her stomach flat, as Arla meant to do. She just moved around a lot, Arla had heard her explain to other women, and she didn't think about her weight. Arla was average height, neither heavy nor thin. She had unusual eyes but she didn't look at them often nor dress them up with makeup. She thought of herself as anonymous-looking and she dressed like a prep-school boy in tailored clothes and cotton shirts. She wondered if Harriet felt around her as she felt around shorter women—out of proportion and a little protective.

Arla took her suitcase from the back seat of the car, and Harriet carried it to the house. There were honey locusts on the front lawn, tall skeletal trees that seemed at first to have grown at random in a pleasing sequence, like the fading tulips that defined the path to the house. The locusts cast shadows on the white clapboard and let patches of brilliant sunshine through in places. They framed the front entrance and made the lawn seem larger than it was. Arla saw two giant stumps on the far side of the lawn and wondered if Harriet or Carl or an act of nature had arranged the convenient amputations.

The house was Federal with a Greek Revival wing that held the kitchen and pantry and, upstairs, the guest bedrooms. There were more bedrooms, a library, the living room and dining room, across the house. It had once been an inn and then had been in the same family for the next hundred years. The proportions of the rooms were at once generous and rigorous. The uneven wooden floors slanted, the plaster ceilings sloped from age and amateur repairs, but there was nothing cozy about the house. It was beautiful, Arla thought, but she had never stayed long enough to grow comfortable there or accustomed to the startling landscapes seen through the bubbly window glass.

Carl was lying on the couch in the kitchen reading the *Times*. He was a heavy-boned man, just Harriet's height, and he had a high, broad forehead that shadowed his brown eyes. His hair was almost silver, faded as the pale blue of his shirt. When she'd first met him, Arla was sure Carl didn't like her. He seemed to look at her from far away with neither judgment nor interest. He reminded her of an old cat who'd found a comfortable spot on the hearth and who saw others only as possible interruptions. Carl was impeccably kind and, on several occasions, had gone out of his way to help Arla. She had come to accept his seeming indifference and demonstrated affection, though she still found his manner disconcerting. Carl looked up when the women came into the house and said, "There you are. We thought you'd fallen off the road."

Arla looked at her watch—she wasn't late at all. "I ran over a bird," she said, "but I didn't fall off anything." She kissed Carl's cheek and he squeezed her arm above the elbow.

"Well," he said. "As long as you're here."

Carl stood and turned on the lights over the stove and the sink. The kitchen faced east overlooking the river, and it was almost dark by afternoon. Iron racks over the kitchen counter and stove held a collection of copper pots and pans and elaborate dessert molds. From the high ceiling hung bunches of dried herbs and strings of onions, garlic, and peppers. Arla wondered if it was the same string of peppers or if it was changed each year. Carl set the kettle on the stove and said, "It's four. Shall we have a very late lunch, tea, or early dinner?"

"Dinner, I think," Arla said. "I'm exhausted. I want to eat too much and fall asleep early."

"We could make pasta," Carl said. "And pesto.

There's just enough basil. There's lettuce for salad, too. The garden's just getting going."

"Luckily for us, I've been marinating chicken all day," Harriet said. "We'll have that. By the way, Carl, I'm thinking of leaving the tulips in the ground this year."

"I hope you like white tulips," he said.

"I like the colors as much as you do," she said, "but it takes five years or more for them to lose their color. We could all be dead by then."

"I doubt it," Carl answered. "I see a long and dreary life ahead of us."

"Surrounded by white tulips," Arla added. She had never liked their quarrelling, nor the way she interrupted them and tried to smooth over their differences.

After dinner, they sat in the kitchen drinking coffee. They talked about common friends in the city and about Arla's work. As soon as she returned to the city, Arla had to start a new project. She was busier than she had been for years, though summer was supposed to be a slow time. Carl's gallery would close for August, as usual, and he planned to be in the city only two days a week during July. They had it all worked out, Arla thought, their lives scheduled and packaged. They seemed safe, she thought, at least safe from uncertainty.

Harriet stood and stretched her long arms above her head.

"We'll spend all day tomorrow in the garden," she said. "You want a suntan, don't you, Arla?"

"You never moved to a bigger apartment," said Carl, "after all that looking."

"I told you," Arla said. "It gets harder and harder to think about moving. And the apartment is large enough for me, really. It's only crowded when someone else is there."

Later, Arla lay in the single bed under the pretty quilt with its design of little girls with watering cans. It was not easy to fall asleep. In the large, sparsely furnished house sounds echoed, and she could hear noises and creaks that might have come from outdoors or in. Though Carl and Harriet's room was at the opposite end of the house, Arla could almost hear them talking and laughing. It might have been the river, it might have been birds, but she fell asleep trying to distinguish their words or the reason for their laughter.

Harriet assigned Arla the lettuce and carrots for thinning, and she worked in the strawberry bed. The garden—larger than Arla's apartment—was a marvel of planning. Harriet had arranged the vegetables and herbs not only according to type, height, and companion planting requirements, but also by weight of leaf—the airy asparagus, the broad, enthusiastic squash—and by shades of green and color of flowers. It was exhilarating to be in the garden and to walk along the foot-wide, hay-mulched paths.

"No matter how I feel," Harriet said, "I come out here and I'm all right."

"And in winter?" Arla asked.

Carl stayed in bed all morning. Once Arla thought she

saw him looking out an upstairs window, but she wasn't sure. At noon when the women went inside, they found that Carl had made lunch for them. On the kitchen counter was a watercress salad, wine from the night before, a loaf of bread, and a platter with slices of roast beef. In a glass bowl there was yellow mayonnaise. Carl talked, as they ate, about homemade bread and mayonnaise, as good here as in France, and about the ochre of the yolks of real eggs. He looked around the kitchen and said, "This is the most beautiful room in the county."

"How can you say that?" Harriet asked.

"I can say it," Carl said slowly, "though I haven't been in every room. I still say it is the most beautiful room in the county. And it deserves a toast."

"I'm not opening another bottle of wine," Harriet said. "We're running out and you won't be bringing any back from the city for a week."

Carl bowed his head as if he agreed but when he raised his head Arla saw the ugly smile on his face.

"You're so impoverished, Harriet. The most beautiful woman in the county."

Harriet looked down at her plate and Arla thought, seeing her mouth pursed, her eyes closed, that Harriet was about to cry. Carl was looking up at the ceiling, and for a moment they seemed to Arla to resemble figures on a Swiss clock—man and wife enter, bow, curtsy, and return to the dark inside the clock. When Harriet looked up, she was smiling.

"Have you seen all the women in this county, Carl? You're exaggerating like mad today."

"Mad isn't a word I would use," Carl said. "We have two cases of wine in the cellar and you refuse to open one bottle."

"Open it yourself," Harriet said.

"No. I refuse to drink disapproved wine."

"Carl," Harriet said. "This is silly. Drink. I'm going back to the garden."

She stood, put her plate and glass in the sink, and left the room. Arla finished what was left of her sandwich as quickly as she could, then looked up at Carl.

"I'm going back to bed," Carl said.

"There are days like that," Arla said.

"Sweet of you to say so," Carl said. "I don't mean to be dramatic, Arla, but there have been months like that in my life."

By late afternoon the women had worked their way through the garden so they were close enough to speak.

"Will you stay here all summer?" Arla asked. "Don't you go to Europe every year?"

"There's too much to be done," Harriet said. "Carl doesn't realize it, but those ochre yolks come from chickens who like to eat every day. And the garden will be ruined if we leave it. He's talking about going to France for three weeks. It would be a relief."

"You wouldn't go with him?"

"I hope not," Harriet said, wiping her forehead with the back of her hand. She left a dark smudge that traced the fine line of her skull around her eyes. "We have the money for one person to go really. I don't even like travelling in the summer. Paris in the summer! I like to get away in the winter."

"So you'll travel in the winter?"

"No. That's when Carl can't leave the gallery. I would only want to go to some island for a few days, which is too tacky for Carl's tastes. I'll be right back," she said. "I'm going to the barn for some mulch."

When Harriet returned, she arranged the fresh hay between rows of herbs. Then she began thinning the small plants of thyme. The fragrance of the pinched leaves came to Arla and she looked over at Harriet. Her face was unlined as if it were marble. She had once told Arla that too many habitual expressions made a face old before its time. Arla felt her own face set in its usual work pattern—eyes squinting, jaw tight. She had been away from Harriet too long for the kind of talk they'd had in New York over the phone or at chance meetings. Arla wanted to ask her what was going on with her and Carl but she had certainly been away too long for that. She was puzzled by what she had heard but she knew that exchanges between couples didn't mean only what they seemed to. They were part of a larger dialogue, and Arla knew she never heard the whole of it.

"Who was that friend of Carl's?" Arla asked. "The one who lived near me downtown."

"Ben Fine," Harriet said, looking up from her row.

"Didn't he kill himself? In some strange way?"

"Yes," she said. "He shot himself in one of those shooting galleries in Times Square. It was strange in a way. What made you think of Ben?"

"I was thinking about when you lived in New York."

41

"He and Carl were lovers," Harriet said, "if that's what you want to know."

"No. Not exactly."

"I'm sorry, Arla," Harriet said. "It doesn't matter at all anymore. Carl left him for me and he felt terrible alone. That's all. I'm sorry to be in such a bad mood, but Carl's been drinking too much and I have to do everything for him. You never met Ben Fine, did you? We didn't know you then."

"No," Arla said. "I never met him. I didn't meet you and Carl until after he was dead, I guess. I'm sorry I asked. I never really knew what happened."

"You might have liked him," Harriet said. "He drew beautifully. It was the only thing about him that didn't annoy me."

Arla went upstairs, took a bath, and lay down on her bed. She fell into a light sleep. Her room was above the kitchen, and through her sleep she could hear Carl and Harriet talking every so often and she heard the sounds of cooking. Guests were coming for dinner, another couple who lived nearby. Arla had never met them. They would all eat that night in the dining room at the long harvest table. The white candles would be lit in the iron chandelier.

Carl and Harriet's house was to Arla a distillation of every country house she'd ever admired. She would have liked a house of her own and a garden, not as elaborate as Harriet's. But she could never live by herself in the country. Harriet thought she was alone but at least she had the illusion of Carl for company. The thought of renting a place for the summer near Harriet and Carl's depressed Arla. She would buy another air conditioner and put it in the living room. She would stay in the city the rest of the summer. The only feeling of being alone she liked without reservation was being alone in Manhattan with everyone else scattered at the beach, the mountains, or in Europe. She looked forward to seeing signs on shops: "Closed for July and August."

"The most beautiful room in the county," said Carl. "If I say so myself. Since I didn't design it, I consider myself within reasonable bounds when I say it's the most beautiful room in the county."

Harriet and Arla smiled at each other across the wide table but changed their expressions quickly before Carl noticed. Actually, Arla thought it unlikely that he would notice much of anything. The candlelight was dim and he was drunk. In any case, the room was beautiful and the food he and Harriet had prepared was fine. The wine the guests had brought sat uncorked, waiting for them to drink.

Arla said, "We should make a thorough tour of the county, Carl, and then we'll know if it's the dining room or the kitchen that's the most beautiful room in the county."

"It's sweet of you," Carl said, "to volunteer to drag from house to house along these back roads, but I think, Arla, we can rely on my taste."

"I do," she said.

It was the first time she'd spoken since they'd sat down to dinner. The guests were named Sam and Pat, and she couldn't remember or hadn't been told which was Sam and which Pat, though one was a man, the other a woman. They'd asked her detailed questions about the block they used to live on in the city, but since they'd lived in Brooklyn Heights and Arla never went there, she couldn't answer them. Then the guests and Carl and Harriet had talked about gardens and mulch, what a bad year it was for rain, about neighbors and the weather. Arla wished someone else was there who was, like herself, a stranger. In the book she'd just finished illustrating there had been a tale that ended, "Be content with what you have." It had been difficult to find an image for that moral. Arla had settled on a drawing of a shepherd boy on top of a hill overlooking a prosperous and fertile valley. The expression on his face, as on hers at this moment, was of someone making the best of a situation.

Harriet picked up a large wooden salad bowl that was next to her. She mixed the salad and was passing it to Arla when the sound of a click went through the room, a loud and sudden noise that caused Harriet's hands to falter on the bowl. She would have dropped the salad if Arla hadn't reached out and steadied the bowl. The click was duller than the crack of a bone, broader than the sound of typewriter keys. It was not a metallic sound nor did it seem to be the resonance of wood against wood.

"Damn that thing," said Harriet.

"We want to be alone," said Carl. "That has followed us all the way from the city. We were naïve enough to hope it was the radiators, but, no, it came with us." He looked at the ceiling comically, as if he would locate the source of the sound and go for it. "Much as we don't want it with us."

"I never heard it in New York," Arla said.

"That's your misfortune. Or fortune. That apartment was perfect except for the click."

"You never mentioned the click when I was going to rent that apartment," Arla said.

"Who mentions clicks?" Harriet asked.

"It throws me," Carl said. He turned to the guests and explained, "It throws me off. It's so loud."

The other guests looked at one another, uncomfortable, unsure whether to laugh.

Arla took some salad on her plate and passed the bowl along.

"It's a nice crisp sound," she said. "I've never heard a sound quite like it before."

"Unique," Carl said. "Very original," to the ceiling.

"Well, it's a lot nicer than some people I know," Arla said. "I wouldn't mind having a click."

"I don't think you 'have' a click," Harriet said. "It's more like being married."

That night while washing her face, Arla noticed how high the bathroom sink was. She could see her eyes and nose in the mirror above the sink but not her mouth and chin. Carl must have put in both mirror and sink to suit himself and Harriet, she thought, and not for the convenience of their guests of normal height. That was his prerogative, she knew, but it made her feel left out. "Click," she thought, and pictured a flat duck with a metal target on its side. Click. She hadn't realized the guns in a shooting gallery could do any harm.

In the morning, Arla and Carl drove to get the Sunday *Times.*

"Sorry I was so testy last night," Carl said.

"You're always a little testy," Arla said. "I don't mind."

It was another beautiful day. The fields they passed were high with grass and wildflowers. Arla was happy to be out driving with Carl, but she didn't want to talk.

"Harriet refuses to leave here in the summer," he said. "Speaking of being testy. She's a pain in the ass about it. I want to go to France with her. We always have a good time there."

Arla's impulse was to recite the argument against travelling that Harriet had given her the day before—chickens, money, garden—but she stopped herself. She had less and less desire to know what the differences were between Harriet and Carl. Arla's opinion, which she wouldn't voice, was that Harriet should go. She wished there were someone urging her toward France, but, she thought, to be fair, if she were Harriet and the person were Carl, her feelings might be different.

"Why don't you go alone, Carl? You have friends there."

"I hate being alone in hotels. I hate being alone anywhere. I don't know how you stand it."

"How is it for you when you're in the city three days a week?" Arla asked.

Carl looked over at Arla and smiled. "Fine. It's all right."

Arla couldn't tell if this meant that he didn't mind or that he wasn't alone.

"I'm the one earning the money," Carl said. "If I want to spend it, we should spend it. She thinks we'll live forever and that we'll want to do these things when we're sixty. She's getting weirder all the time. She never puts more than two dollars' worth of gas in her car."

"Yes," Arla said. "I asked her about that once."

"It's the flip side of thinking we're immortal. She says she might die anytime and the money would have been wasted."

After he bought the paper, Carl drove back to the house the long way through the woods. Arla began to look forward to packing her bag and driving home to the city. She would leave a few hours earlier than she planned in order to get to an early movie. She looked forward to being alone on the drive but dreaded unlocking her apartment. The first fifteen minutes alone always depressed her. Listening to her married friends, Arla knew there was nothing necessarily enviable in marriage. She would not have liked to discuss the time of departure or to make other adjustments in her desires, small or large. She didn't want Carl and Harriet's marriage nor any other she could think of. She wanted a companion and an entrapment of her own, though she had no faith that she would do any better with hers. Even tempered by reality, even though she told herself she was foolish, it was what she wanted and its absence made her sad.

Arla was ready to leave after lunch and when she came

down the stairs carrying her bag, Carl was there to kiss her goodbye.

"Bon voyage," he said. "Maybe I'll call you one of these days in New York."

"Please do," she said. "Everyone's leaving but me." Harriet walked her to her car.

"I decided to leave half the tulips in the ground," she said. "And store the other half in sawdust."

"That sounds reasonable to me," Arla said.

"It probably sounds like a lot of crap to you," Harriet said.

She touched Harriet's arm and wanted to hug her but Harriet was so thin and stiff that Arla thought an embrace might snap her.

"I miss you in the city," Arla said. "I wish I had my own tulips to worry about with you."

"Sometimes I wish I were back in New York," said Harriet. "But I'm happy enough here. It doesn't do to think very much about whether I'm happy or not. This is it for me."

They agreed that Arla would come back for the Fourth of July. As she drove away, Arla saw Harriet walking across the lawn to the house. Whether her head was bowed from despondency or to look at the tulips, Arla couldn't tell.

She had left the country early enough so that traffic was light coming into the city. Only a block from her building, Arla found a parking space that was good until Tuesday. As she walked home, Arla saw that the streets were almost as empty as she liked them in summer. The only stores open for blocks were a delicatessen and a florist. The florist was bringing buckets of mixed bouquets of roses and tulips into his shop, getting ready to close for the day. Arla thought of buying a bouquet as she passed, but the tulips reminded her of Harriet and seemed more problematic than desirable.

She didn't go to the movies after all. By the time she had opened all the windows in the apartment and unpacked her bag, she decided she'd be going out only to avoid being alone. She opened a can of tuna fish and made a salad from all the vegetables in the refrigerator so that it would be ready when she wanted to eat.

In her studio, Arla meant only to read her mail, but she picked up the text for her next project, a fantasy book about birds. She recalled the bird she'd killed on her way to the country and she sat down at her drawing table. Arla opened a bottle of black ink and began to draw the bird. It took shape on the paper before her and turned back to look at Arla, as it had from the road. She made a fine line for its beak and wondered if it had been a gull, so far from the sea, then reached to dip her pen into the ink. The click resounded as it had the night before but now it was larger, crisper, and more spirited, as if it had gained energy on the trip back to the city. Startled, Arla looked down at the drawing and saw a splatter of ink obscuring the bird's head.

BURIED TREASURE

All morning we'd worked side by side, and we were nearly finished gardening when Gwen told me to look. A green V.W. had come up the drive and was pulling in next to my truck. A few years ago, everyone drove V.W.s, but now no one did, and all I could think was Who is dropping in like this, unannounced and unexpected? It had taken me the years I'd lived in that place to get it straight with people—Don't come without calling first.

Gwen, who watches birds without the aid of binoculars, narrowed her eyes in her farsighted way, sized up the visitor, and said, "It's Vance. All dressed in white." I could just make out his shape as he left the car, spotted us in the garden, and started walking toward us. "He's wearing something swell around his neck," she said, showing off a little.

"An albatross," I suggested, though he was more like the wandering Fool of the tarot deck than the blighted Mariner. My hand felt loose on the tool I'd been using and I wanted to heave the hoe across the chicken wire at Vance. Instead, I rested it against the fence and squatted on the ground to tighten the laces on my sneakers. It was a blistering July Fourth weekend. I was wearing cutoffs and the loose top of an old bathing suit, and looked like a Saturday gardener, while Vance was pristine, coming across the freshly cut lawn toward the garden. His skin was tanned the light honey color I'd always envied.

"I told you he'd be back," said Gwen, who loves to be right.

"I have no memory of your telling me that," I said. "But if you did I never believed you."

He was close enough now to speak, but he kept his eyes on a point between Gwen and me, beyond the hills and the sky. He brought his gaze first to me, then to Gwen, as if in blessing, though his look was more blank than benevolent. "Vance," I said, and wished that I didn't want to reach across the fence to touch him.

"How are you? Good Lord, it's been a long time," said Gwen, sounding more friendly than I would have predicted.

"How long *has* it been?" I asked, not really expecting an answer. He'd never been one for reminiscing, and as for the future, he wanted each day to be new and unpredicted. Though the three years of absence were easy to add up, he hesitated, so I said, "You've never been good at keeping track, have you?"

"Not really. I don't know how long, Nessa. The garden has certainly grown."

"Would you like some zucchini?" I offered, as though he were a neighbor come to call. "Basil? Are you staying with your cousin?"

"Yes," he said, and smiled at my row of questions. He touched the fence with his hand and said, "I'd like . . . whatever."

Past the tomato plants Gwen and I had mulched with hay, past the new rows we'd dug for second-crop lettuce and arugula, just at the dill, I caught the sharp sweet odor of the herbs. The rows were so orderly. Sometimes at sunset I came out to gaze at the garden while my cats sat beside me, watching the darkening sky. I tried to be as peaceful and unmoving as the cats. A central bed of red nasturtiums I'd planted for cutting was the only point of contrast in all the green.

"Are you and Charley here for the summer?" I heard Vance ask Gwen. It was just like him to assume that everybody has all the time in the world to do as they like. Gwen has a private practice in New York—she's a psychotherapist—and Charley's a lawyer. They lead scheduled lives, and their weekends are planned to the minute, like military campaigns, their arrivals and departures announced weeks ahead. The day before they come, I travel from town to town, gathering up their favorite foods—raw milk from Jersey cows in Hoosick Falls, meat and New York State cheddar from the butcher on Railroad Bed, eggs from our friend Molly—as if Gwen and Charley were invalids who needed coddling. I don't ask them to share those miles of country so often travelled alone. I indulge Gwen and Charley, even beyond what I consider proper for my best friends. Their country time is so short, their visits are so infrequent. And, after all, I moved here myself to avoid such crammed weekends, such a doling out of country minutes.

"Not for the summer, just the weekend," Gwen said to Vance. "But it's a long weekend, you know."

I cut Vance some medium-sized zucchini with my pocketknife. They were tasty enough, and I was holding back on the babies. I picked mint for tea before I returned to the fence, where Vance and Gwen stood talking. He was slouching, hands in pockets, as if he were waiting for a train. "Notice the black stripe," I said, and I handed the shiny squash across the fence to him. I pulled back my hands before they had a chance to touch his. "A new variety," I said.

"The place looks fine," Vance observed as the three of us walked slowly across the freshly cut lawn to the slate patio he and I had started together. I didn't say that Charley, now napping in the upstairs guest room, exhausted after mowing the grass, had finished the patio one Labor Day weekend. Of all the things I'd forgotten and remembered about Vance, it was his voice—light and sweet—that left me first and most permanently. I'd tried to catch it many times, but failed to hear him say again the things I wanted to remember. Later, I would have been happy to hear him say anything.

On the patio, Vance chose a black wrought-iron chair that faced away from the house, out over the valley, and Gwen settled into a white Adirondack armchair. She has red fuzzy hair that forms a halo around her face. Her skin is thin and sprinkled over with pale freckles. The night before, I walked from the garden to the house and saw Gwen washing dishes at the sink, framed by the arched kitchen window. She had the look of a pure Dutch beauty. When I told her this, she looked pleased, then said, "I'm no beauty, Nessa. I'm much too fat."

"I'll make us iced tea," I said, leaving Gwen with Vance on the patio. Once inside the house, I changed quickly into a T-shirt and skirt. While the water heated, I stood at the kitchen window, watching Gwen and Vance.

She was asking questions. He was responding. I was still surprised at seeing him do anything normal. He had been so silent with me always that it was like living with a storm cloud that hovered but refused to burst. Yet I'd missed Vance for three years solid. The day he went, I searched the house for something he'd left behind, sure that he was still there with me. It was only in the last months that the missing had lifted and I'd stopped seeing him in the rearview mirror whenever I was stuck in traffic, stopped thinking he was the thin figure just passing out of view around a corner. When the tea had steeped, I fixed a tray of glasses, mint, and ice, and I carried it all out to the patio.

". . . Morocco and Tunisia for a while," Vance was saying. "Then my mother sent me to Greece. My brother Guy—" He turned to me. "You remember him, Nessa? The young one. He got himself into a mess there."

"What kind of mess?" I asked.

"Opium. Now he's back in New Orleans."

"Did you come straight here from Greece?" Gwen asked. She accepted the glass I gave her and held it away from her chair, letting it drip onto the green-and-black slate.

"No," Vance said. "I was in Spain. Before that Italy, in a house like this. Out in the country. I helped some people rebuild a stone tower. Then Boston again."

"You've got to see this house inside," Gwen said. "It's a miracle. Not anything like the place you left."

I looked at Gwen to check if she was trying to reproach Vance for leaving when he did, at the first frost of

my first winter in the house. She must have been reminded, as I was, of the times I phoned her in the city
and told her of the silence of that winter alone, of the
times I looked around and saw only half-finished rooms,
gray skies, and white fields. To all this she would say
firmly, as if her words were a bitter dose that would cure:
this was what I'd wanted, after all; what I'd saved for and
asked for; this was my house.

But sipping her iced tea, chatting with Vance, Gwen
looked bland and innocent. "You two were sleeping on
the porch back then, weren't you?" she asked.

"Yes," Vance answered for both of us. "I liked the
porch—sleeping there at night."

He half closed his eyes, dreamy and calm, and I said, to
break his reverie, "I liked it a lot less when the temperature dropped. I'm tearing off the porch this summer."
And when he twisted around to look at the screened-in
porch sitting there, waiting to be taken away, I explained,
"It ruins that elevation. The house will look better from
the road."

He settled himself again in his chair and went on as if I
hadn't spoken. "I liked sleeping listening to the animals."

"That's because you sleep like a turtle," I said. I had
had too many nights of insomnia out there to be senti-
mental.

"Did I sleep too long?" Charley called down from an
open bedroom window.

"Up just in time," said Gwen. "Vance is here for a little visit."

"I'll be right there." Through the screen on the bedroom window I could just make out Charley's form. He looks so much larger in the country—almost bearlike—it's hard to imagine how elegant he is in his business suits. He takes a special pleasure, I think, in his metamorphosis.

Gwen stood up, setting her glass of tea on a table she and I had made from a tree stump and a slab of wood. "Never mind," she called to Charley's window. "Stay where you are." And she left me on the patio with Vance.

The view from the patio out to the Taconic Range was hot and still; a mist lay between the hills, where the streams and lakes were cooling off the air. The many times I'd imagined Vance's return, it had taken place in shadow, at dusk—never in bright sun, the two of us sitting politely, drinking iced tea while our glasses dripped.

"How's the barn?" Vance asked, as if inquiring about my health or the status of a mutual friend.

"Same old same old," I said, wanting to tell him a lot had changed.

"I left some things by your horse barn," he said, and gave me a sidelong glance I remembered as the prelude to a secret or an announcement.

The place had come with a large hay barn, and I meant to do something with it someday. Meanwhile it stood empty, just beyond the house, the boards turned silver with age and the weather. There had originally been another barn—an L-shaped horse barn—but the boards and beams were sold by the last owner to a contractor in Connecticut. Only the old sills were left to rot.

"The fact is," Vance said, and he smiled as if he were

enjoying a good joke, "I left my beads there. Underneath the foundation. I didn't know where I was going or for how long. And I knew they'd be safe here with you, Nessa."

"If I'd sold the place or moved . . . You took quite a chance, didn't you?" I said.

"You'd never sell."

"I thought of it."

"And if you did . . . I meant to come back, but one thing after another happened, and then my brother being sick . . ."

In the heat of the day, Vance and I abandoned our cool spot by the house. We crossed the lawn and climbed the wooden fence at the barns, and the smell of the mown grass clung to us as we looked over the foundation of the horse barn. What had been a tentative patch of wild blackberries had taken over. The barnyard was a jungle, impenetrable and threatening. All I could see in the thornbushes was the outline of the foundation, its beams barely visible. The thought of the beads buried in there made me want to laugh. Vance had been so careful with his precious beads. He'd selected them one by one from the hoard of a grave robber in Lima, smuggled them into the States from Mexico, then carried them here to New England. The few times he chose to show them to me, he was sure to roll them up afterward in ancient scraps of cloth and tuck them back into separate pill jars. The jars he folded among his clothing, in the leather satchel that was his only baggage. The beads were ancient clay, shaped like yo-yos and spindles, and figured in geometric designs I couldn't read. There were carnelians and turquoises also, and thin tubes of beaten gold, some rubbed so fine there was barely any gold left, only the shadow of the tube. The nights he took the beads out to show me, Vance spread them on the quilt that covered our bed on the porch, and we looked at them by candlelight while animals cried in the dark and moths beat against the porch screens.

I tried to think of a word to mitigate the thorns, but Vance wasn't waiting for my sympathy. Without a word, he turned and walked back to the house. When he came back, he had a shovel and a pickaxe, a pair of clippers and a saw. I leaned against the fence, and Vance took off his shirt. While my arms had grown hard and strong from gardening and splitting wood—just from living in the country—he was bone thin, down to nothing. Still, we looked alike, Vance and I, the coincidence of our coloring and the shape of our heads holding true: both of us black-haired and stern-looking, both brown-eyed and grim. He laid his white shirt by me on the fence post and attacked the thornbushes with the clippers until the sweat burnished his honey skin. I stopped myself from offering help, but I could not stop myself from watching.

Clipping systematically, the blades beating a tattoo, Vance exposed the outline of the southern corner of the foundation. He trampled down the stubs of the bushes, then looked past me to the sky and turned slowly in place, his eyes fixed on one spot as he moved, like a ballerina taking care not to make herself dizzy. It might have been a magical Peruvian ceremony of discovery; when the turning stopped Vance said, "Has anyone been here? Something's changed, Nessa."

"Just us chickens," I answered. "I didn't move the beams, if that's what you mean."

He looked again at the sun as if it had betrayed him, and then he set aside the clippers. With the pickaxe, he started to gouge a narrow trench around the farthest edge of the foundation.

"Digging for buried treasure?"

Charley and Gwen stood outside the fence on the lawn. They were dressed for fishing—old dungarees and T-shirts, flannel shirts with extra pockets sewn on. Over one shoulder, Charley had slung Gwen's canvas bag. Before they'd married, she'd used it as an overnight bag, occasionally rinsing the removable lining of nothing more serious than spilled makeup. Now the lining had to be washed regularly to remove the scales and smells of their catches. Charley carried three rods. Mine was an old fiberglass job I'd found at a yard sale, much like one I'd had as a child. Theirs were fancy graphite—Christmas presents they'd given each other. Gwen was holding a tin can, which she tipped to show me the worms she'd found in the compost heap. She also had a six-pack of beer. We'd been planning to go fishing when the day cooled off, in a pond at the top of the hill. The pond belongs to my neighbor; all spring he'd been complaining that the bass he'd stocked it with were multiplying faster than they were growing, and I'd offered to weed out the edibles for him next time Charley and Gwen visited.

When he heard Gwen's voice, Vance stopped working, but he didn't speak. "Vance left some things behind," I explained. "His beads—he's digging for them."

"Great," said Gwen. "Where's your map? Is it written on parchment?"

"I don't need a map," Vance said stiffly. "I remember quite well where I put them."

"I'll be up the hill in a minute," I told Gwen. "I want to see the treasure recovered."

"Suit yourself," she said.

"Don't be too long," added Charley. "The light's getting to be about right." They waited another moment, and all four of us just stood there, Vance with his pickaxe, I on the fence, the two of them ready to fish. Then they moved off up the hill and out of sight.

On his hands and knees, Vance made his way along the corner of the foundation. In between the roots of the thornbushes the soil was dark and rich with composted wood and ancient manure. It might be only a matter of minutes before he came up with the treasure. Then he would leave again. On his last day with me, he told me in the morning he'd be gone by night, and when at midday he disappeared I imagined he was taking a last long walk. He must have been burying the beads. He must have planned it out deliberately, the way he did everything. In the bedroom—the one room he'd finished—he'd spent hours inches from the wall, smoothing over the smallest adjustments he made to the plaster. Now I thought, If only he'd told me then that he was leaving those beads behind, if only I'd known there was something of value on the place; it would have made a difference.

Vance got up from his knees and walked to the fence, where I waited. I could smell the earth on him, he was so close. He brushed at his white trousers, leaving traces of blackness.

"Everything's shifted," he said, sounding as sad as I've ever heard him.

"Try again," I suggested, for I wanted to be kind. "Perhaps it's only deeper than you remember."

He sighed and resumed his careful work. Extending the trench on both sides of the beams, he clipped farther along. In the fall, I'd prune back the bushes to see if they'd produce better berries, and I'd invent a way to sift the roots from the soil he was digging, to use the soil on the beds of strawberries and asparagus. My house was finally finished. Every room, upstairs and down, had smooth walls painted pale shades of gray and white. I had closets, I had bookshelves. In winter I laid Oriental carpets in every room and the colors—ruby, coral, sapphire, emerald—shone in the hard northern light. It was time to live for my garden.

The heat of the day was past, and I wondered how Charley and Gwen were doing. I wanted to be drinking beer and talking with them. I didn't like staying with Vance, watching him as if my day would have been empty without his unexpected reappearance. With his hands he was feeling along the edge of the L—first one side, then the other. He had dug about a foot down and I could tell by his expression—fixed and dissatisfied—that he was finding nothing. I didn't want to lose a minute of him, but I forced myself to say, "If you don't need me, I'm going fishing."

"Of course," he said, politely. "I'll be out of your way any time now. I'll come up to the pond to say goodbye."

I doubted he'd climb any hill to speak to me. I didn't believe I'd ever see him again. I took a last look at Vance, who leaned on the pickaxe as if waiting for me to be gone, as if he had a surprise tucked up so far inside himself that he'd forgotten what it was.

Flies buzzed the water's surface in lazy waves. The light wasn't quite right, and the fish weren't biting. Gwen had drifted the six-pack off the pond's broken-down pier, and the three of us stood around the egg-shaped pond, far enough apart not to cross our lines, near enough to hear. Charley had caught one bass right away, but it was less than six inches and he'd thrown it back. Squinting into the woods, he said, "Maybe there aren't any big ones."

To answer him, I pointed to the shadow of a bass, enlarged by the water surely, but large enough. It stayed smack in the center of the pond, where we couldn't quite see it.

"I told you he'd be back," said Gwen.

"But three years later?"

"I never said when."

"You also never said how long he'd stay once he got back."

"How long could you possibly want him to stay?" Charley asked. Before I could answer, his attention was taken by a faint pull on his line. I rarely fish. It seems to me a matter of luck—not skill or control. Gwen and Charley disappear for days to fly-fish for trout on the Battenkill, and for years they've talked about taking a long vacation in Scotland to fish for salmon.

I got one definite strike, Charley got two, and then I saw Vance coming over the hill. He carried his shirt and the zucchini, and his face showed streaks of dirt and sweat. There was a smudge near his mouth that looked like a bruise.

"The pirate's revenge," Gwen called. "Have a beer."

"No. Thanks," Vance said. "I came to say goodbye."

"Any luck?" Charley asked, keeping his eyes on the water.

I reeled in my line, laid my rod on the ground, and walked over to where Vance stood. "It's gone," he said. Then his voice softened. "The earth must have taken it back. Thanks for letting me try, Nessa."

"You're taking it very well," I said.

"Ah. I shouldn't have left it so long, should I?" Already he seemed to have gone, his intended departure and past absence becoming the same thing to me.

I said, "Give my regards to your cousin."

"Good to see you, Nessa." He waved his hand and called goodbye to Charley and Gwen. I watched him walk all the way down the hill to his car. I stayed watching until his car was out of sight.

Even when the sun was lower and the air just right, the fish didn't care for us. Gwen and I gave up and sat together at the edge of the pond, observing the movements of the dragonflies as they teased the surface of the water.

"I wonder if he's lying," Charley said from the opposite bank.

"What about?" I asked.

"Once a sucker, always a sucker," Gwen said. "Charley means, Do you think Vance found the stuff and didn't tell you?"

"Why would he do that?"

"So he wouldn't have to give you any. That's the obvious reason. But I don't know. . . . I never understood why Vance did anything or why you put up with him."

"I didn't put up with him," I said. "I loved him."

"I wish I could believe him," she said. "Because if the beads are what you think they are—I mean pre-Columbian and Peruvian gold—we should be out there digging."

In a little while, Charley gave up and Gwen dumped the worms. "I'm returning them to the earth," she announced, and we collected our beer cans and walked down the hill. Without saying we would, we walked straight to the barnyard and saw that dirt was banked carefully around the beams and that the clipped branches were stacked on one side. Vance had covered his tracks.

Charley went over to the foundation and tested his weight against the beams. "Archimedes," he said. "Most likely, the beads are buried too far under to reach. Give me a crowbar and I'll move these things."

"Once we've lifted them," Gwen said, "we'll find the stuff. I know we will. Where was he looking, Nessa? Just in this corner? Around the other side? Do you see any other places he might have been digging? Maybe he waited for you to leave so he could slip his hand under and lift them out."

"For Christ's sake," I said. "He was looking right there. He really thought they were there."

"Well, I hope they still are," Gwen said. "I hope we find them. Three-way split."

"That's stealing," I said.

"Don't be a Goody Two Shoes," Gwen said. "This is piracy."

"Maybe a woodchuck got them," Charley said, and he climbed the fence to join us.

We started toward the house, and to keep the peace I said, "Yes, maybe."

"Never mind," said Gwen. "We'll try in the morning—it's getting dark anyway, and I'm hungry."

"I'll pick some vegetables," I said, and left the two of them at the door of the tool shed.

In the garden, I gathered up the tools Gwen and I had abandoned when Vance arrived. For dinner I'd pick lettuce and baby carrots and dill. We'd dig in the morning for treasure, but I hoped we wouldn't find it. Let the beads return to the earth; let Vance vanish empty-handed. Gwen had turned on the kitchen lamp, and the light that fell from the window into the evening looked as though it were made of gold. My first summer on the farm had been so green. Vance was with me and I'd believed—as I believed no longer and didn't want to—that the feelings I had for him would be maintained over a lifetime. It was different now, with nothing staying the same from day to day, not even the barn against the sky.

I stood and surveyed my garden to see if there was anything else I wanted. Over the smooth expanse of lawn I saw a shadow moving as if it were coming straight to me. I smiled. I nearly laughed. Then I turned and picked the smallest zucchini, the ones I'd saved out for myself.

SWEETHEARTS

At times we couldn't get together on the simplest things. One Saturday morning, for example, we were working on the house when Grahame and Paula arrived to see the progress. Visitors were rare—we didn't have a phone and most of our friends lived north of the river, too far away just to drop by. Sometimes old neighborhood women stuck their heads in the door, but they withdrew quickly when they saw James or me inside. I don't know what they expected or hoped for. The ground floor had been a butcher shop for years and perhaps they thought a new shop would open to save them the long walk to Camberwell Road. That day, James was concentrating on wiring, not listening to what I was saying. He'd been distracted since he bought the house, bearing the householder's pack of worries and dreams. But when he saw it was Grahame and Paula come to visit, James' face opened like a child's into the widest smile imaginable. "Grahame," he said. "The very person I need."

Grahame's glasses were cutting into the side of his nose and he looked rumpled, but perhaps he was only feeling the heat. I hadn't seen Paula for a few days, and it seemed to me she'd swollen in that small absence. She looked as if she'd give birth that morning, though it was three more weeks before Augusta was born. The weather was hot for London, even at the peak of summer.

"I'll carry you upstairs, or Kathy will," James offered,

and it seemed someone might have, but Paula just smiled and followed us slowly around the house, commenting that it looked—and we looked—as if we'd been working our brains out. We'd ripped all the plaster from an up-stairs ceiling—a disaster. Originally the plaster had needed no more than patching, but on his birthday, a clear dry day, James took off five ranks of roof tiles to repair the gutter. We were living then at his sister's, in a room she used for boxes and suitcases full of clothes she would neither wear nor part with and for a certain kind of dust that made me sneeze. The room had one large win-dow overlooking a cemetery, all that was left of a church bombed during the war. James and I were making love the night of his birthday, drunk and not caring about any-thing else. It was the way we'd been when we met: both on holiday, both ready for each other. Then we heard the rain. James stopped and lay still, listening. "Damn," he said, and I said, "Damn," and it rained all through the night and the next day, as much as it does in a normal summer month in England. The ceiling was completely ruined.

By the time Grahame and Paula dropped by for their Saturday tour of inspection, James and I had been haul-ing and tearing for weeks just to get where we were be-fore the rain. We had no car then, so Grahame volunteered to drive us to the ironmonger's to pick up plaster and a few tools we needed. We were ready to leave when James and Grahame lingered too long by the entrance box. Paula and I stepped outside, looking in the shopwindows along Tabard Street, and in no time we were blocks away, along a route I'd never taken before.

I always, or nearly always, felt awkward with Paula. We saw each other often, first because of James and Grahame's long friendship, then because I was new to London and had few friends. She had sharp features and skin that flushed easily, a face I could imagine in a tapestry of a medieval lady. Paula and Grahame were childhood sweethearts. One evening they'd shown us pictures of them at sixteen and nineteen, awkward, hands just touching, standing before an old-fashioned cottage somewhere in the country. They had been married three years—three times as long as James and I had even known each other—and sometimes they seemed more like brother and sister than husband and wife. They seemed completely together for life, which was hardly true of James and me. Some mornings when I woke James for work, still hurt by something he'd said the day before, something he'd no doubt forgotten, I was ready to tell him I was leaving. He'd smile at me first thing, kiss me, and ask, "What's the time? How's the day?" as if the day wouldn't start without my answer, and I'd let go of my morning feeling and give myself over to another day with James.

I fell in love with James within a week of meeting him. He'd struck me as a lucky person and cheerful, though months of living with me and owning his house were wearing down his good nature. I was five years older than James and thought it was high time for luck and cheer. I made the move to London and James with less anxiety than it usually took me to decide what to pack for a weekend away. James met me at the airport and took me straight to the house he'd found in Southwark. He didn't have the keys, so we scaled the wall of the neighboring garage and walked across the roof of a covered yard to get in through a paneless second-story window.

"Do you like it, Kathy?" he asked as he led me through the dusty rooms. It was nearly sunset and we could barely see each other—only the outlines of the walls and the furniture that had been left behind. "Is it hopeless?"

"The size is right," I said. "It could be done by one person with not very much money. If you're patient."

It would have been the moment for us to acknowledge that there were two of us now—with very little money, but two nonetheless. Nothing was said, and from the start it was James' house, his first place of his own—not his parents', not his sister's, not the public school he'd attended from age eight on, not ours. He took heart from my encouragement. Within weeks he bought the house and we began work.

Paula was flushed and uncomfortable and swollen by the baby, but she looked almost picturesque, walking along the dusty street. I looked more like James' assistant than like his lover, my hair flattened by a work kerchief, my skin covered with a layer of plaster. But on our walk I forgot all that, and was content to be out on the street and to notice Paula's blue-and-white checked dress rise to draw a graph on her belly, then flap in front of her like the opening of a tent.

We crossed Great Dover Street—past the tough pubs and tired council flats, past the playground and the Catholic school—and found a square that stopped our talk of babies and men. Unlike much of Southwark, the square was unbombed and Georgian. The houses bordered a simple lawn and three giant trees, a wrought-iron fence and locked gate signalling the privacy of the park. The square was serene and solid, not only in its architecture but in the sense I got of stable lives behind the unadorned white façades. Paula remembered that in one of the houses lived a famous writer of thrillers—or he had at last reading of some Sunday supplement. "He cooks in there as well," Paula said. "He writes cookbooks on how to prepare food if you're in a hurry." We trailed around the square, looking into every kitchen window, but each was so distinguished in its way that we couldn't decide which was his.

Then Paula and I made our slow way back to James' house. It was a small building, plain as a pancake except for the plate-glass window and the tattered green awning that shaded it. The front was faced with green tiles right up to the black glass sign—POWELLS. The equipment from the butcher shop was still there—two long marble counters, white-tiled walls, stainless-steel bars and hooks for hanging meat. In the window was a stainless-steel exhibit shelf that had held who knew how many lambs and cows, how many selfless chickens. Now the only remnant of that past was a faint smell of meat in one corner, resisting us no matter how we swept and scrubbed.

"How could they?" I asked when we reached the house and saw that the car was gone, the door padlocked three times. James might have left without me, but Paula looked so vulnerable, so heavy, standing there so pregnant. I opened the locks and let Paula into the white-tiled room. The nearest chair was two flights up and covered with plaster dust, but I offered to bring it to Paula. She smiled and asked, "Is there a piece of paper? I'll leave Grahame a note and go home on my own."

"I'll write James," I said, and the two of us leaned against a marble meat counter and composed our notes on scraps of bills I'd found. We stuck the notes to the door and locked up the place again. Paula's train didn't stop at our station but at Elephant and Castle, a half mile away. I asked if she'd prefer to walk or take a train and switch lines. "I think I'll make the walk," Paula said.

We hadn't got very far down Borough High Street when Grahame's car pulled up beside us.

"Silly girl," Grahame said to Paula. "We've been driving in circles, looking for you."

"Nearly went home without you, mate," Paula said.

"We came back," I said, "and you were gone."

James looked at his watch. "Did you expect us to wait all day? The ironmonger's closes in less than an hour. Saturday, my dear," he said in his mother's Cornish way, and he opened the door for Paula and me to get into the car.

"Are you all right?" Grahame asked on the way to the store. "Would you rather I took you straight home?"

"I'm fine now," said Paula. "We'll go home after this, if you don't mind. I'm a bit heavy on my feet."

The store was crowded, and before a clerk came to wait on us I got a chance to price soap holders and bath racks. James and the clerk talked until each finally understood exactly which tool was needed. The clerk produced it from a large wooden cabinet with drawers of all sizes. Unlike me, James was always confident in stores that you could get what you wanted as long as you made clear exactly what that was.

Paula almost fell asleep on the short ride between the ironmonger's and home, and we agreed to meet the next evening for a movie—early show, at her request. James and I stood in front of the butcher shop, waving goodbye, until he started to open the door.

"Why didn't you wait for us?" I asked.

"We were nearly in the car and then you were gone."

"But you could have waited a little longer."

"You walked out without a word. And we did wait. Honestly."

Later, when James was up on the roof, chipping away with his new tool, I took our notes from the door and read them.

Paula's note said:

Couldn't find you. Returned home. See you. P.

And my note read:

Took short walk with Paula, then came back and where are you? Walking Paula to underground. K.

James was probably right. We shouldn't have gone off like that. But he might have waited. I wondered if I would ever be like Paula—slow, patient, large as a house; carrying something so precious to James that he would wait, put me first; would carry me upstairs and lay me down to rest.

REAL ESTATE

There's one place or more in every piece of wood that's ready to give in to the wedge; a hairline crack betrays it. From the end of September, mornings that felt like December, I woke, dressed, and worked on making a woodpile. Once I had a large enough pile, winter could do its worst; until then, the season and I would be like boxer and trainer—I the boxer, winter the one in the car, yelling at me to keep up my pace.

One morning in mid-October, I thought I heard the phone ring. Sometimes the sound of metal against metal—sledge against wedge—rings out and the last reverberations sound like the telephone. Sometimes in the quiet between strikes of the sledge, I hear my neighbor's phone down the road, and I think it is my own. I didn't recognize the voice on the line until he said, "Janet. It's me. Beau. How *are* you?," and I said, "O.K. It's a little cold," and then remembered Beau.

"How are *you*?" I asked. It had been a hundred years since we'd spoken, a little more than three since we'd had a farewell cup of cappuccino on Broome Street, across from the laundromat we both used.

"I'm better than I've ever been," said Beau. "I was up your way last Sunday. I called and called. Where were you, girl?"

"Around somewhere—but where were you? What were you doing here?"

"I've been about an hour from you all summer off and

on, visiting friends, house-sitting. Until Sunday, I had no idea we were so close. I saw ten acres of land advertised in a local paper—a fabulous piece, some schoolteachers own it—and I thought I recognized the name of the town from that postcard you sent me. Then there you were in the phone book. I loved the land, but I didn't get to see what the view was—which is crucial. It rained like hell all day Sunday, don't you recall? I couldn't see two feet in front of me."

"And you were out walking land?"

"Was I ever. I even had a friend with me, if you can believe it."

I thought I could hear "lover" inside "friend," and that echo recalled the days when Beau and I used to meet for laundry and coffee, and recount our affairs to one another. He had so many more than I that I stopped telling my stories after a while, but Beau, always polite, would ask, "How's Bobby?" or "How's Chris?" dragging up a name I'd mentioned maybe once, weeks before. I used to tell him to stop invoking the dead.

"Did your friend drown in all that water?" I asked.

"Oh, no. Not at all. But, as a matter of fact, I cut my thumb on some damned thornbush. My whole hand's sore. Listen, I'm house-sitting for only one more week, and I really want this land. How about if I come up on Thursday and we look at it together? I'd value your opinion." He described the location of the land and told me the asking price. He said that at long last he was going to use his famous savings and start to build. Beau had always talked about his dream house, but I never really thought he'd get to it. His New York life seemed to suit him, for Beau was open to a new chance meeting him around every next corner.

I told Beau Thursday sounded fine with me, and he said he'd call as he left for my house. He was dealing directly with the owners of the land, and they were in a hurry. They needed the money to continue renovating a Victorian house they'd bought. It was a marvellous house, he said—twenty rooms or more.

Whenever I went into town to the bank or the post office, I passed by the land I now called Beau's land. There had been a real-estate agent's sign on it as long as I could remember. As Beau had described it, his land was in back of a grove that bordered the road. I added that spot to the other sights on the seven-mile drive—the hairy cows and the trees nearly bare. The cows were telling me how cold it was going to be, and my swollen cats—pregnancy, I thought at first, or worms—were growing their coats for winter. It was the start of my fourth winter, and I was more bold than I'd been the first year, when I sealed up the house with storm windows and weatherstripping right after Labor Day. Now, getting toward November, a note taped to the refrigerator ordered me to wash and put up the storm windows. I'd do it, I knew. If winter wasn't entirely to my liking, that didn't change the fact that it was coming.

Beau had always been a great traveller, and the savings he'd mentioned were from the voyages he'd made as a merchant seaman. He'd been around the world, and when I knew him he was using the wages from his sea life and from working at Abercrombie's every Christmas to travel more. A portion of his savings he never touched. Beau kept a cheap apartment on Prince Street as his base. He spent his time in New York doing research for his trips, and he filled his apartment with maps and travel books. Beau spent little money on himself, really—he had few clothes and splurged only on books or records. He had a way of doing without until what he wanted was given him.

The summer I was leaving New York, Beau began to show a greater interest in his apartment. He built in a bed and storage cabinets—"the most ingenious subletters couldn't possibly break into them"—and, in the middle of that hot August, he ripped out the bathroom. With scrap lumber and a few boxes of tile a friend had given him, Beau rebuilt it entirely. I met him on the street with his parents when they were up from North Carolina, right after the completion of the new bathroom—a task I suspected Beau undertook for his parents' sake. His father was shorter than Beau, and his mother even shorter than that. They resembled Beau mostly in that they were dressed as neatly and conservatively as he. His father was a little seedier than the other two, but I could be making too much of the odor of his cigar. At our meeting, Beau's mother complained of the heat and dirt in New York. They'd just moved into a new house, and she missed the central air-conditioning. His father was more courteous. He mentioned how impressed he was by the Bronx Zoo and the quality of the food at the restaurant Beau had taken them to the night before. Later, when his parents had left town, Beau showed me a color snapshot they'd given him of the two of them standing by some extravagantly blooming azaleas outside their new house. "I swear," Beau said, "that house is a replica of the one they lived in before, only the other wasn't brick."

Beau didn't call Thursday morning. I waited inside until eleven and then went about my business: I raked leaves, I split wood. He called at two in the afternoon. "This is the first chance I've had," he said. He'd been in a hospital emergency room all morning. The thorn that had cut him when he'd walked the land had been poisonous—his hand had swollen so he couldn't close his fist, and a black line crawled to his elbow. He wouldn't be up to see me that day. He'd call when he could make the trip.

By the time Beau called again, it was November. His hand had healed, though it had taken weeks and made his return to the city "boring and impoverished." Beau was earning his living as a carpenter or typist—wherever he could find work—and his infected hand prohibited both professions. He was coming upstate Friday, he said, and staying for the weekend. He wanted to see the land again; in fact, he wanted to close the deal. Would I walk the land with him Saturday?

It had snowed a few days before, but the snow was gone. The cold was bearable, and it was still possible to walk the land. I told Beau I would ask a friend who was a part-time real-estate broker to come with us and tell him what she thought of his deal.

He arrived on time Saturday, though the car, he said, was almost dead on arrival. He looked the same as ever to me. "I have to be back tonight at my friends'," Beau said as we went into the house. "That's their car, not mine. A mixed loan, I can tell you. . . . What a charming kitchen. I knew your house would look like this. My land being near you makes it all perfect."

Since we hadn't been in touch for three years, "perfect" seemed an excessive description. I assumed he'd thought of calling me, as I had of him, but we were mostly neighborhood friends, so I let it pass. I had lost touch with all the people we'd known in common, but Beau had kept up with everyone. While we ate a lunch of cold veal sandwiches, he told me about old friends in New York. Only a few were the same, or at least living in the same place with the same person, working at the same job. The rest were scattered all over the map.

I asked Beau what else he'd done to his apartment.

"Everything," he said. "Every inch. I can't do another thing to it."

After lunch I called my friend Molly, and we arranged to meet at the land. Molly and I had been to college together, and twelve years later we were neighbors, both having come, by chance, to this same part of the state. When Beau and I drove in off the main road, Molly wasn't there, and Beau said he wanted to go up alone. I said I'd wait for Molly. The lane we'd driven in on had seen better days, but probably not much better, and Beau said there was another three-quarters-of-a-mile walk back to his land. He took a canvas bag with him and his jacket, and hiked out of sight. I sat on the hood of my car, which was still a little warm. The lane ended on a rock bed near a locust grove, and that grove seemed to me perfect for a house. Its perfection didn't matter, since it wasn't the land in question. I waited ten minutes or so before Molly drove in.

"Sorry I'm late," she said. "I couldn't get away. Does the land start here?"

"No. Beau went ahead, but he told me it begins after the barbed wire, at that fence post."

We walked as far as we could, and at the fence post headed straight up a hill. When we reached the top, we looked around for some sign of Beau. Molly spotted his things lying on the ground. There was a notebook, Beau's canvas bag. His jacket was laid over some dead bushes as if the bushes were a valet's arms.

"He's making himself at home already," I said.

"Moving right in," said Molly.

Minutes later, we heard Beau's voice calling out, "Welcome, welcome," and we saw him standing on the crest of the next hill. "Fantastic," he said when we reached him. "This seals it. This is the place for me. A view is so important." Molly nodded and so did I. "I want to thank you for coming," Beau said to Molly.

"That's all right," she said. "I'm always interested in looking at land."

They went off to walk the boundaries, and I went back to the first hill. The view was spectacular—east to the Green Mountains, northwest to the Adirondacks, with all the land divided into fields and woodlots. The hill itself was overgrown, and I avoided touching the bushes—they might have been the ones that had poisoned Beau's hand.

"I want an absolutely simple house," Beau said when he and Molly had climbed back up to where I stood. "Almost a glass box."

"Better make it double glass," I said. "The wind will cut on this hill."

"Yes," he said. "I wonder how the sunsets are."

"Are you planning to build this yourself?" Molly asked. "Have you a great deal of money to put into this?"

"Lord, no," Beau said. "Just my famous savings, scrimped and stored away over the years. My father said he could negotiate a loan from our hometown bank. But this will be Shoestring Hill."

He looked so pleased with himself and his prospects. I knew Beau well enough to put the story together now: an ad in the paper, the discovery that nearby was someone he knew, and, presto, he was about to sink all his money and his energy into this land. I'd done something of the same thing myself three years before, and though I wanted to tell him the news of being in debt and bone-tired, I remembered how it felt to start something. I said, "It really is beautiful here, Beau. You should be able to get a bush hog back here to clear all this away easily enough."

"Do you plan on electricity?" Molly asked.

"I guess," Beau said. "I mean I'd like to heat with solar and wood and all that, but I still would need electricity."

"To build you would. Unless you planned to use hand tools or bring in a small generator."

"Well," he said. "I guess you begin at the beginning, with electricity."

"I hate to say this," Molly said, "but, first of all, the price isn't great for this. Reasonable but not unusual. You're going to have to build a road, and that's not so bad, except for that rock bed. But the electricity is going to cost."

"How much would it be?" Beau asked.

"I don't know exactly. Let me pace it out and then I'll be able to estimate. I'll meet you back at the car."

Molly went off down the hill, counting her paces out loud. We couldn't hear her anymore after twenty paces.

"How would you keep the place going, Beau?" I asked. "Would you try to find work around here? Live here all the time?" I was going to ask if he would give up his apartment on Prince Street, but that seemed too delicate a question.

"I don't know what I'll do," Beau said as he put on his jacket. "I just know I need something solid. You can understand that. That's why you did it, isn't it?" He put the notebook inside the bag. There was a slight indentation in the dead grass where his things had been.

We caught up with Molly and listened to her count the paces the rest of the distance to the cars. When she finished, Beau asked, "What's the good word?"

"Not so good. I'm sorry. It would be a lot of money. Really a lot. They'd have to blast to get a pole in this rock, and that costs. Even if you get permission to go through the piece in front, it's still a long way. It would probably amount to twice the purchase price."

"Are you sure?" Beau's expression didn't change much at this news—his smile hardened slightly, then his

91

face smoothed over again. Beau had always said if you don't count on anything, you don't get disappointed.

"I'm sure," Molly answered.

"Well. That's that," said Beau. "I suppose. Those folks who are selling it didn't mention this problem."

"They wouldn't," I said.

"Maybe they didn't know," Molly said. "I'm sorry, but that's what it costs here for power. If you were crazy about the land and didn't care about money, or if you didn't mind taking twenty years before you finished the place, that's something else. You could buy it and just hold on to it until you had the money to build. It's up to you."

"No," Beau said. "I guess not. I guess it isn't what I thought."

We stood there talking a little longer. Where we were, you couldn't see the sunset, and it was getting cold. We talked about windmills and alternative sources of power, and then Molly said she had to pick up her daughter at the babysitter's. Beau thanked her, I told her I'd call her the next day, and we backed our cars out of the lane.

By the time we got back to my house, it was dark. Six o'clock on a November night, it feels as if January will happen by seven. I noticed I hadn't brought in the wood I'd split before Beau came. The fire in the wood stove would be out by this time and the living room would be cold.

"I'd better go," Beau said. "I don't think the lights always work on that damn car."

"You're welcome to stay here. There's a real guest room—wallpaper and everything."

"I promised I'd get back there tonight with their car."

"Come in for coffee or a glass of wine," I said. "I'll get a fire going, and then we can sit down."

In two trips, there was wood by the stove and more stacked in the woodshed.

I renewed the fire and got out glasses and wine while Beau washed up. He came out of the bathroom with his face scrubbed and held one arm out to me. I saw the line, faint red by now, going up his arm.

"It was an omen, Beau. It's just as well the electric was so expensive," I said. But that didn't feel like the truth. It was too bad about the whole thing, too bad he'd ever seen the ad; still, I felt as if I'd done him a wrong turn and deprived him of something he wanted.

"That land was going to be my big present to myself," Beau said. "Next Tuesday's my birthday. You know, I'm not a kid anymore. I was ready for this whole deal. Settling down."

We sat at the kitchen table, and we kept having one more glass of wine until there was no more wine left. By then it was seven-thirty and pitch-black. I started to make coffee, and Beau said, "I may build a dish rack like yours. Hanging it on the wall would give me the other half of my sink. Do you really live here all alone? All the time?"

"People come for weekends," I said. "Not much in the winter. I go to the city sometimes. When I need a sudden lift."

"Shock is more like it. You should call me next time you come in. We'll go out and make some noise. Don't you have any animals? I thought all you country folk had chickens and ducks and geese."

"I have three cats," I said. "But they're outdoor cats. I'm allergic to them."

"They've invented a new kind of cat for people with allergies," Beau said. "Bald ones."

"Bald people with allergies?"

"Bald cats. I swear."

"Who would want a bald cat?" I said. "The whole point of cats is their fur."

"Same as that land," Beau said. "Who wants land you can't get to or build on?"

"Do you still want it?" I asked.

"I went against all my rules and counted on getting it."

"For your birthday," I said.

"Not just my birthday, the rest of my life. Lord. Enough of this."

Beau used the phone to call the people he was staying with, to say he was a little late starting. They told him there was a party going on, and that gave him new energy. He was excited now at the thought of driving back, less tired than he'd been since we left the land.

"Come with me to the party," he said. "I'll get you back tomorrow somehow."

I said no, that I had too much to do the next day. I don't like parties, but so many things happened to Beau at them that he always tempted me with his invitations.

The car wouldn't start at first and then it did.

"Thank Molly for me," Beau said. "And thank you.

You were wonderful. Without you, I'd be the owner of that dark inaccessible land."

"Sounds like a national anthem," I said.

"Call me when you come to the city."

I watched the car go down the road until I couldn't see the lights anymore, then I walked back to the house. Beau wouldn't buy land, I thought, at least not soon. I wondered how I looked to him—splitting wood and waiting for winter, thinking about bald cats and hairy cows— and then I figured he probably hadn't even noticed. Though years had gone by and I lived in a different place, everything seemed the same as it always had. I wondered if the party would be any good or if, in fact, it would still be going on by the time Beau got there.

THE
KINDNESS
OF
STRANGERS

E dward found May on the last cold day of winter. He spotted her in his neighborhood bar, and noticed first that she was comfortable there. She sat with one iceless drink, an ashtray, and cigarettes in front of her—an organized person. The bar, at the end of the afternoon, filled with smoke, and Edward could see himself and May reflected dimly in the mirror. Christmas decorations hung over the mirror and would probably remain there until next Christmas.

Though he had been fine when he came into the bar, Edward began to feel shaky. The smell of steak from the grill was getting to him. He leaned on one elbow and decided that as soon as he could move he'd go back to his apartment, take some Valium, and sleep. He was wondering how he could meet the woman down the bar, when he thought he saw her look at him and move her fingers in a quick salute. The basketball game on the TV above his head grew louder, then softer, and Edward thought he'd better do something about getting home before he fell off the stool. He stood, and while he was fumbling in his pocket for money she was beside him. They left the bar together.

She told him her name was May—a name Edward associated with prints of women in long dresses and floppy hats. May carried a cowboy hat and wore an Army jacket that was too large for her. In the street light her hair and eyes were a faded khaki color. "You look sick," she said. "That's why I followed you out. I thought I'd be sure you got home all right."

"That's not far," said Edward. She sounded Southern or Western to him, and he felt as if he'd left Manhattan without knowing it. Now that they were out on the street, she seemed less than a good idea. All he wanted to do was fall asleep and wake up feeling better. "It's nice of you to worry, but I live right over there," he said, and he pointed to the large apartment building across Broadway. "I can just about make it."

"Of course you can," May said. "But you sure look green." Together they turned and walked the half block to the corner. "Is there anyone to take care of you once you get there?" May asked.

Edward thought of lying, but he said, "No."

"Then come with me." And when he shook his head, she said, "Goodness. You looked easy to me."

"That's me," Edward said. "Sick and easy. A wonderful way to be."

He didn't feel easy; he felt unemployed and difficult, and he wanted to be left alone. Still, this was the first adventure to offer itself in he couldn't remember how long. He thought of his empty apartment and the fact that it was Friday, and he said, "I have always relied on the kindness of strangers."

He followed May's lead and they crossed Broadway. As they walked by his house, Edward wondered if the night doorman noticed him passing. Halfway between Amsterdam and Columbus, May said. "Here's where I live." The building, a renovated brownstone, was more high-toned than he'd expected. More than ever, Edward felt that he wanted to be sick in private.

"I must have a fever," he said. "Maybe I'd better go home."

"Don't be silly," May said. She led him down three steps and opened an iron gate. She let him in the apartment door, and went back outside again. He heard the gate slam and then the door. "Go right in," she said. "I'll open the couch for you."

A long hall led past a closetlike kitchen into the living room. In the widest part of the hall was a table, one side against the wall. One wall of the living room was brick, two were painted gray. The fourth wall was glass and opened to a dark garden. The couch May had spoken of was blue and there was a double bed in the room covered with a piece of blue-and-white homespun and pillows of red and blue. "This is a nice place," Edward said. Expensive, he thought. He walked to the end of the living room and looked through the glass doors. He could make out pots stacked upside down. When he turned back to the room, he saw that May had the couch open and white sheets spread over it. There was a pair of striped flannel pajamas laid out.

"I haven't worn pajamas since I was twelve," he said.

"Well, wear them or not. I always like to wear pajamas when I'm sick."

"Will they fit me?" he asked, picking them up and holding them to his chest.

"They're my brother's," May said. "They fit me and him. They fit everyone. Go brush your teeth. I'll make some tea for you."

Edward reflected as he obeyed her instructions that she must be an exceptionally nice person to take in a sick stranger. He wondered if she always picked up strange men from bars, then thought he wasn't so strange, though a look in the bathroom mirror—pajamas, hair sticking up, toothbrush protruding from his mouth—showed he wasn't exactly a prize peach. She'd picked him, though, and that made it a benign act. He wouldn't hurt anyone and she must have seen that.

Edward had a terrible night. May settled him in his bed, gave him tea and club soda, used the bathroom herself, and then disappeared into a room he hadn't noticed at the street end of the apartment. When he found a comfortable spot on the bed, he would sink into it too far and feel sick again. He'd probably picked up a bug in the Szechwan place where he'd had lunch. He could taste the Garlic Eggplant.

Edward fell asleep at dawn. When he woke, it was three o'clock and he was alone in the apartment. There was a glass of club soda next to the couch—the ice cubes were half melted—and a fresh pot of tea, still warm to his touch. He could see a piece of paper—a note from May—propped up on the table across the room. He was probably not sick anymore, he thought, but when he stood he became dizzy. The note read, *Went to store. Back at four.* He was stuck there. He had no keys, and it wouldn't be right to leave without double-locking the door.

There was a time in his life when Edward would have

searched the apartment, quick, before May returned. He would have liked to read her letters and diaries, but he decided against that course. There were no bookshelves and he didn't see even one magazine in the kitchen, living room, or bathroom. A look through the half-open door of her bedroom startled him—there was someone asleep in the bed—but it was only tangled sheets and covers.

Edward returned to the couch. He should get dressed, he should be ready to go home when she returned, but he didn't move. Instead, he lay there and waited for May. He thought about the office where he used to work, the long boring afternoons. He didn't have high hopes for another job. In three months, he'd sent out one hundred and twenty-five letters, and planned to send out more. He thought about a morning the summer before when he'd woken up next to a woman and couldn't remember her name.

At five, he decided May was not a punctual person. He saw his clothes folded neatly on a rocking chair. He got out of bed and looked in the wallet, but his thirty dollars was still there. It wouldn't make sense for her to take money from him and leave him in her apartment. He heard her key in the lock and wondered how he could have been suspicious of her.

"Sorry I'm so late," he heard her call out. Lights came on in the hallway, above the table. May carried two large grocery bags.

"I thought I'd make soup for you," she said as she set the bags down and took off her Army jacket. "You feel better, don't you?"

"I feel a lot better than last night," Edward said. "It must have been the Chinese food I ate."

"It could have been anything, in this city," May said.

"You're not from New York, are you?" he asked.

"Maybe nobody's from New York," May said. She walked back to the hall and Edward could just see her hanging up her jacket. "It's warm out," she said. "Sixty degrees." She was wearing a white turtleneck and jeans and cowboy boots.

"I'm from New York," Edward said. "Right here in the neighborhood. We lived on Eighty-first and Central Park. Two down from the Beresford." He saw that May was interested, and he asked again where she was from.

"The Midwest," she said. "No place you've ever been."

"I went to graduate school in Chicago."

"That's not the Midwest. That's Chicago."

Edward wondered if he should get dressed and go. The pajamas were wrinkled, and the bed bore the imprint of his body in several places. But it was already Saturday night, and he was getting through the weekend almost without noticing it. Since he'd stopped working, weekends were longer than ever.

May told him she wanted to change the sheets. She gave him another set of pajamas, baby blue with darker blue piping. When Edward returned from the bathroom dressed in the blue pajamas, he felt almost well. He saw that May had closed up the couch. He thought that perhaps this meant that they would sleep together in her dark bedroom or in the double bed in the living room, but May said, "I closed the couch until you go back to sleep. I thought you would feel less sick that way," so he knew nothing was expected of him. She gave him a fresh glass of club soda, and while she made dinner he sat and watched the six-o'clock news. He saw an Arab leader and a fire in Brooklyn, and had a sip of soda.

"The weather's turned," May called out from the kitchen. "I won't need to wear a jacket tomorrow, I'll bet."

Edward was sorry winter was gone, but he called back, "That's good. It's been cold long enough."

He could look for a job forever and not find one, and in the spring it would be worse. He thought of the Green Mountains, where he'd spent his last two vacations, and wanted to crawl back into bed. He flicked off the TV and reached for a book he noticed on the floor. It had been hidden by the couch in its open state. The book was an atlas; it was well worn and had the marks of a favorite book.

Edward let the book open where it wanted to and saw, circled on a map of the United States, New York, Philadelphia, Cleveland, Detroit, and Boston. Boston was circled in blue and the other cities in black. There was no mark farther west than Indiana. He felt May watching him from the kitchen door. When he looked up, he couldn't tell from her expression if she was displeased with him. "Are these places you've been?" he asked.

"Some of them. I didn't mark the towns below a hundred thousand population on the big map. Only on the state maps. And I mark where I want to go next in blue. My route. I want to go everywhere."

"This is your diary, then," he said. "I'm sorry."

"Don't worry about it. I left it there on the floor."

"It's your floor," he said. "And you didn't know I was going to be here."

"It's not my floor," she said. "It's the apartment's floor," and she returned to the kitchen.

When May was ready, they sat at the table with a certain formality. She had set straw placemats beneath blue glass bowls. The soup in the bowls was clear; Edward could see the pattern of the mat through his soup. A round of carrot and a sprig of parsley skimmed the surface.

"Have you ever been sailing?" he asked.

"No," May said, "but I love the water. I grew up landlocked."

"All that corn," he said.

"Corn and wheat. But I wasn't on a farm. My mom grew up on a farm, but it had to be sold when my grandfather died."

"How old were you?" Edward asked. He took a taste of his soup. The flavor was a little bland to suit him, so he added salt and pepper and tried it again.

"Seven, maybe. I forget exactly. We went down there to close the place up. We had an auction for the furniture—I had an orange soda at that auction, I remember. Then we sold the cows and gave away the goats and the geese. It was mostly a chicken farm and the chickens were pretty worn out. My dad and I must have killed a hundred and fifty chickens. My mom cleaned them and froze them."

"Why didn't your brother help your father?" Edward asked.

"I forget where he was. I don't remember everything about it. It wasn't the Slaughter of the Innocents or anything. It was just chickens."

Edward put down his soup spoon. He'd eaten too much too quickly.

"Maybe you should lie down again," May said. She was looking at him as if she were measuring him, and he wondered how she'd looked at the chickens.

"I'll be all right," he said.

"There's no reason to keep sitting up. I can see you from here if you go lie down. We could keep talking if you wanted."

He obeyed. He lay on the couch and pulled a blanket over himself. He did feel better lying down.

"Where do you work?" Edward asked, as May cleared the table.

"In a shop off Broadway. In the Eighties. I make clothes for people, and I sell candles and rolling papers and pottery."

"How long have you had it?"

"I just work there. The owners are away for a few more months and they let me take it over."

"Do you work Sundays?" Edward asked. If he was better the next day, the least he could do was take her out to dinner—if he could eat by then.

"Monday's my day off."

They watched TV until eleven o'clock. Edward kept changing the channels, but it didn't seem to matter to

May if they watched a detective series or a game show. They watched fifteen minutes of a beauty pageant, and she told him she'd been in a Miss Indiana contest when she was seventeen and hadn't won. Her skin was so smooth it reminded Edward of a doll. Only her hair looked real to him—not curled, not smooth or shining, but hair like grass.

In the morning, Edward felt better but still weak. He was awake before May and lay staring at the closed door of her bedroom, thinking about making love to her. He didn't think he felt much desire for her. Still, making love would seal the accident of their meeting—though he wasn't sure he wanted that, either.

When May finally got up, she went straight for the bathroom and didn't look his way. He dressed quickly, and by the time she was out of the bathroom he'd closed the couch and was sitting at the table, unwashed and waiting for water to boil in the kitchen.

"I'm making tea for you," he said.

"You don't know where anything is," May said. "You go wash and I'll do it."

"I'll go home this morning," he announced later, while she made breakfast. Again the table was set; she'd put red napkins next to the blue glass bowls and cups.

She said, "O.K."

He waited for a sign from her that she expected something else from him, or that she wanted him to stay, but she only asked how many minutes he liked his eggs boiled.

"Three minutes if you're starting with boiling water," he said. "Six if you're starting from scratch."

He stood at the kitchen door and watched her prepare the eggs, toast, and another pot of tea. "Shall I take you to dinner tonight?" he asked. May looked at him quickly, then down to the eggs again. Edward thought he'd seen enthusiasm in her eyes, and he said, "The Russian Tea Room. Have you been there?" He hoped that she would accept so that he could impress or excite her, and he hoped that she would refuse. Dinner there would be a good half of his unemployment check.

"I've never been there," May said. "Do you think we could get in? Sunday night?"

"I'll try," he said. "Give me your number and I'll call if I get a reservation."

"I'll call you," she said. "Or maybe we could just meet back here. Six or seven. I don't like talking on the phone."

At the table, while they were finishing their eggs, Edward felt a breeze hit him. May had left her bedroom door open and from where he sat Edward could see curtains billowing by an open window. "I knew a girl in college who was allergic to winter," he said. "She reacted very strongly to the cold. Her skin cracked at the joints."

"Don't tell me about her disease. Please," May said. "I can't stand hearing about sickness."

"You don't seem to mind that I'm sick."

"That's different," she said.

"How different?"

"I took you in for reasons of my own."

This sounded flirtatious to Edward and he started to

smile, but she wasn't flirting. Her face was the same as ever, she wasn't asking anything of him. "What reasons?" he asked. "What possible reasons?"

"My own. And what you said the other day about the kindness of strangers. That's how I live. I believe in that."

Later, as they left the apartment together, Edward thought that he should tell her that line was a quote, so she wouldn't give him credit for it, but he didn't. May locked the door and the gate. The sun was shining. It was warm. Spring had come in two days. "Everything happens so fast in New York," he said to May, and pointed to the sky.

"Some things do," she said, and he wondered what she meant by that. They walked west together to Broadway, and she left him there. Edward picked up a Sunday *Times* from the New Yorker Book Shop and a Danish from Party Cake across Broadway, and then he went home.

All Sunday afternoon, it seemed to Edward his life had passed him by. He had missed the big events of his generation—when Woodstock occurred he was visiting his parents at the Jersey shore; he was in Chicago when the peace marches were in Washington and New York, and in New York when the riots were in Chicago; and this afternoon he could get no one on the phone. He had lived in New York for years, worked for the same company from college on, suffered economic reverses, and he could find no one to have dinner with later in the week, to ask for advice about a job, or even to tell that he'd been sick and now felt a little better. He reached two answering machines in seven calls. One machine played Bach.

After a shower, Edward still felt weak. He opened the windows in his bedroom and living room, and the fresh April air reminded him of the sadness of spring. He looked down ten flights to the courtyard, and he saw a boy shooting a basketball at the space between the lobby door and the second-story window. The boy was red-headed and skinny. His blue ski jacket lay on the ground. Every third basket or so, the kid would trample on his jacket. Why was the boy alone, Edward wondered, and why wasn't he in a playground where there were real baskets to shoot at.

It seemed to Edward he had done everything right all his life, straight down the line, with the best of intentions, and it hadn't come out as he'd expected. He tried to picture May as he'd seen her in the bar. She came from a world Edward didn't know. He couldn't tell what she expected from her life; she was foreign to his experience. He thought about her and, not having read the paper or eaten the Danish, Edward went into his bedroom and slept.

When he awoke, he felt hung over and had a taste in his mouth he didn't like. He looked on the table next to the bed and found some sugarless gum—tutti-frutti—and stuck a piece in his mouth. The powder on the gum tasted like insecticide, but he chewed away, his arms in back of his head, hoping the gum would give him a reason to get up. He thought of the circles in May's atlas. No one could want to go everywhere. He could probably have offered to take her to the Cuban-Chinese place on Amsterdam and she would have enjoyed it just as much as the Russian Tea Room. He took the gum out of his mouth and put it in the ashtray on the table.

He arrived at May's door a little late. On the way over, he'd thought about her name. Perhaps she'd been sent into his life to be an omen of other differences to come. If he could get over feeling sick, perhaps he could get interested in her. He wondered what she thought about spring. He could remember little she'd said except that she had her own reasons for taking him in and that she wanted to travel. He must be getting better, he decided, to take an interest in another person.

He rang the bell outside May's gate and waited. Then he rang again. It was almost seven, but perhaps she wasn't home yet. Then he listened and thought he heard music and voices. He made out the strains of "Queen of the Silver Dollar" and a man's voice, insistent, droning, repeating a phrase over and over. He rang the bell again and this time heard footsteps. The door opened, and the gate.

"The music was so loud," May said, "but Roy thought he heard something." The music was still loud, and when Edward said, "I only rang twice," he had to raise his voice and repeat it. The second time, his words sounded demanding, almost whining. He didn't feel as jaunty as he had walking over. May's face looked different to him, more open, and her eyes looked brighter. It was possible that she was glad to see him but he didn't think that was it.

He followed May through the long hall into the apartment and saw a man sitting at the table where they'd eaten breakfast. The straw mats and red napkins had been pushed toward the wall. An ashtray filled with butts lay on the table, as well as a worn address book, a passport molded into the form of a back pocket, coins of different sizes, and greasy papers that had been folded and unfolded so many times the edges were ripped. To one side, carved ivory rings with black circles incised and rough carved stones and scarabs were heaped together. The man rose to greet Edward and he stood half bent over, bobbing back and forth. He was dark, and his eyebrows grew all the way across his forehead.

He turned from Edward to May. "It's foolproof," he said. "Inside, you understand. You roll the stuff up inside the newspaper. Mail it third class. Fourth class."

"Never mind," May said. "Nothing's that foolproof. This is Edward. Edward, this is my brother, Roy."

"The one with the pajamas," Edward said.

"What pajamas?" said Roy. "I never wear pajamas. I hate pajamas."

Before Edward could pursue the subject, May said, "Have a seat."

He sat and looked at Roy. Probably they weren't brother and sister the way he'd thought she meant, though why anyone would want to pretend to be Roy's sister Edward couldn't see. "How are you feeling?" May asked, and explained to Roy, "Edward's been a little sick for the last few days."

"That's right," Edward said. "She took me in."

Roy nodded.

"I don't know what I would have done. It was a piece of luck that she came along."

Roy nodded again, as if in profound agreement, and said, "I know, man."

Edward watched as Roy bent over the pile on the table. Roy began to sort out the stones and rings into smaller piles of different sizes. Edward thought about the Russian Tea Room, and pictured himself arriving with May and Roy. He thought, No, we'd better skip it.

"You still don't look too good," May said. She squinted to see him better. "You'd better not eat any fancy food tonight." She spoke in her neutral way, as if she'd done her part and he was on his own again, as if the food didn't matter to her either way.

"I guess not," Edward said.

May selected a ring from the largest pile on the table and held it in her hand, palm up. "Look at this," she said. "Roy brought it for me, all the way from Africa. It's from a real elephant's tusk." It occurred to Edward then that—brother or not—Roy was a thief, maybe a smuggler. He was sure of it. He looked around the apartment. The possessions there told him nothing about May, nothing that would prepare him for the brother with the ivory rings.

"How long have you had this apartment, May?" he asked.

"I don't know. A couple of months. The owners come back in another two months." She put the ring on the table and lit a cigarette. She was bored with him, Edward thought. She wanted to get rid of him so she could be with her Roy, who was also looking bored, staring at the table, moving his hands now and then to separate a stone from the herd. Edward could stay just to annoy them, but probably after a while they wouldn't notice if he was there or gone.

He stood and said, "I think I'll have a glass of water and go home." He waited for May to say something. The only thing he wanted from her was to find out why she had bothered to take him in at all, but probably the reason was that May did rely on the kindness of strangers— for apartments, for jobs, to take her home from bars if she looked sick.

In the kitchen, he opened one cabinet and then another, looking for a glass. He noticed on the shelf, around the glasses, a layer of pale-yellow powder. He saw a tin of cockroach poison and thought how the tin had probably been put in the cabinet by one stranger, knocked over later by another. Around the rim of the glass he held in his hand was a film of powder, like salt on a Margarita.

He put the glass in the sink and turned back to May and Roy. He should tell them about the poison, but maybe they knew. If they knew, maybe it was better not to say anything. They were talking softly, planning what they'd do once he was gone. He looked at them sitting across the table from one another. One second they looked benign, then mean; foolish, then calculating. If he could get to the door, everything would be fine. He said, "I guess I'll go now," and moved toward the hall.

They both looked at him, and May raised her hand to wave to him. "Bye," she said.

"Bye," he said. "Thanks for taking care of me."

"You weren't any trouble," she said, getting up from her chair. "Here. I'll let you out."

On the sidewalk, Edward listened to May locking the gate and the door, and he could hear footsteps returning to Roy and the table. It was nothing. She'd had no schemes or plans for him and the adventure was over, except that he still felt sick. As he started down the block toward Broadway, Edward thought he could see the first Monday of spring coming toward him.

FREE
AND
CLEAR

Mike took his vacation upstate in May, right after the mud season. It was a small change, but it counted to him. For the last five years, he'd lived on schedule—two years behind a desk in Fort Myer, then three in New York City, working in the distribution department of a film company. Every August he went to his grandparents' house near Hoosick Falls and returned to work the Tuesday after Labor Day. "Business," he would sing on his way to work, "business ain't nothin' but the blues."

This vacation, Mike brought his guitar, and he intended to rearrange some of his old songs. He was trying to put an act together and was planning a first album. During college, he had performed in some clubs in Boston. Just before he was drafted, he had been trying to get work singing in the Village. It was now so long since he'd performed in public or finished a song to his satisfaction that he didn't tell people he was a singer and songwriter. People in New York knew him as amiable enough, content to float or rise with no more volition than a helium balloon.

He'd spent every summer of his childhood in his grandparents' house, and the happiest Christmas and Thanksgiving holidays. From the time he was five, he had taken the bus by himself to Bennington. His grandfather, D.C., would meet him there and drive him back to the house, which always looked the same to Mike. In the

119

past year, D.C. and Mary had become ill. She died in August and D.C. in February. Mike visited them both in the hospital in Troy, but he missed D.C. at the end. He wanted to be there, but no one called him until it was too late. He was only in New York City, he told D.C.'s lawyer after the funeral. Mike wanted to emphasize both that it was only four hours away and he could have been there and that it was too late now and all could be forgiven. The lawyer replied that it was none of his affair where Mike had been.

His grandparents left him the house and land, and every last one of their possessions, including D.C.'s collection. They hadn't told him they would do that, and Mike wondered if he would have said yes or no if they'd asked. A real-estate broker came by the first day Mike was there and urged him to sell while the market was good. Each time Mike drove into town, he slowed down to glance over at the cemetery. He didn't adorn their graves with bunches of flowers or potted plants. He didn't set a plastic wreath against their stone. He went once to see that the stone was all right, but he didn't stay long.

His parents were retired in Arizona. They wrote Mike a letter telling him to be careful around real-estate people. They asked him to ship them his grandmother's rocker. His father added the postscript: *Real estate is a steady investment but it has its costs.* Mike meant to write a song from his father's advice, but he hadn't gotten around to it yet. He doubted anyway that he could cram it all into one song.

The house was chilled and a little damp; the furnace had been shut off for weeks and it would be summer before the house was dry. When Mike first walked in, he put down his guitar and suitcase and, out of habit, went straight to the kitchen. The room was clean, and when Mike checked the refrigerator he saw that it was empty. Someone had thrown away all the half-finished jars of jam, chutney, and pickles Mary used to take out for lunches at the bleached wood table. He noticed a photograph, tacked up on the wall by the stove so long before that its edges curled over the thumbtacks. He took it down and looked at the back. In his grandmother's handwriting: *Mike as a Cowboy,* and the date, an August day twenty years before. In the photo he stood, one hand steadying his two-wheeler, streamers hanging from the handlebars. He wore a cowboy vest over his plain shirt and jeans, and a toy gunbelt hung from one hip. He was squinting into the camera, starting to form the lines now definite around his eyes. Behind him there was a white picket fence and, propped against the fence, the skull of a cow. Mike had a memory of D.C. calling out to him, "Hold it right there," and of Mary tacking up the picture, but he felt no connection with that serious boy, holding so stiffly to the handlebars.

The first night, he went around to the back of the house where his grandfather kept his tools. He found a hammer and some nails. The toolroom looked and smelled as if cats had been in it, and the tools were scattered with terra-cotta pots on the floor. The light was out in the toolroom, so Mike straightened up by moonlight. He stepped outside and listened to the spring night. There were some sounds missing. The chickens were gone. Mike couldn't remember if D.C. had given them away or sold them, or if he'd mentioned them at all. People in the city forget how noisy the country is, he thought. The storm windows were still up in the house, and if he left the door open for the night air mosquitoes would consume him. He took the hammer and the nails he'd found back into the house. He drove two nails into the parlor wall, side by side, and hung his guitar by its embroidered strap. He stepped back to see how it looked on the wall. Here was the house he now owned, there was his guitar on the wall, and no one to ask if it was all right to have put it there. He felt a small guilt at his act, but in the morning it reassured him to see the guitar.

In Mary's time, the downstairs had been kept dark. Every spring, she applied a fresh coat of varnish to the floors of the parlor and the dining room, and to the woodwork in each of those rooms. For as long as Mike could recall, the parlor walls were covered in light green paper with a silver leaf design. In the middle of the dining room was a round oak table, at which Mike sat the second morning he was there. He tried to compose a postcard to a woman he'd been seeing in the city. He'd met her three weeks before at a party on a Circle Line boat trip around Manhattan. The gaiety of their meeting hadn't been matched since, and when he tried to write that it was great here and would she like to come for a weekend—"I'll pick you up at the bus"—it didn't sound right. He couldn't imagine being with her for Friday night, Saturday, Saturday night, and Sunday. They dated in urban parcels of time, and over the long stretch of a weekend they might have nothing to say. He put his attempts at postcards in the middle of the table and left them there. He recalled a terrarium his grandmother had made, and he went into the parlor, found it, and set the terrarium on top of the postcards. The terrarium contained several specimens of cactus, set in sand. Mary kept the top sealed with a piece of domed glass that magnified the green and silvery plants. When the dome caught what little light entered the dining room, the terrarium glowed and Mike thought that dawn in the desert must look like that.

In the next few days, Mike went through old letters his grandmother had saved and he threw away many of them. Others he didn't know what to do with: those congratulating Mary on a birthday or anniversary, those condoling with her for the death of her eldest son, killed in the Second World War, and for the loss of her father, mother, and two sisters, killed in a car accident in Florida one winter. There was a picture of the son on top of the piano, where it always had been. Mary and D.C. had stood by Mike when he decided to try for noncombatant status in the Army. He didn't believe they had respected him for it or had even listened very carefully as he explained that the war in Vietnam was a different kind of war and required a different response. They stood by him because it was the right thing for them to do, and he had accepted that as good enough. He stopped talking about the war.

It didn't seem right to Mike to throw away the letters Mary had saved, but he didn't want them. He imagined sending them to his mother. It was her dead brother, her aunts and grandparents, but he didn't kid himself that she would appreciate his gesture or that he would ever hear the end of it. He wouldn't have the energy in a million years to put together a package of the letters, much less take the package to Hoosick Falls and mail it. So he made a bundle with the same string Mary had used and he put the letters back in the desk in the parlor.

Every morning, Mike mowed the lawn, extending it another foot or so into the fields that surrounded the house. In the evenings, he sat on the porch and played his guitar and thought about the house. He thought that if he kept the place he would sand the floors, strip the woodwork, and wax it with paste wax. He would steam off the wallpaper and paint the plaster behind it. But when morning came again Mike changed his mind. He was used to the old patterns on the wallpaper. He remembered how cool the dark floors kept the parlor in summer and how formal at Christmas.

Having gone through Mary's letters, he turned to D.C.'s collection. When Mike was a boy, there were several small rooms upstairs. In recent years, D.C. had decided to make a public museum of his collection. He wrote a letter to Mike's father saying that the location was perfect, smack between the horse-racing museum in Saratoga and the art museum in Williamstown. He'd knocked down most of the walls upstairs, leaving one room for Mike when he visited. In the middle of the large space, he set a table that ran the length of the room, and there he laid out the shoeboxes and display cases that contained his collection, which included the planes and trains he'd carved while recovering from a wound received at the end of the First World War. Each model was labelled: *Carved by D. C. Welch while confined to hospital Albany New York.* There were also pearl studs and tobacco tins, harmonicas and kazoos, stuffed birds, can openers, nineteenth-century safety pins and toothbrushes, arrowheads, crushed bullets, a jar of pencil ends, glass from an early Coke bottle, and a piece of a Greek temple. During Mike's childhood summers, D.C. took him to the battlegrounds near Schuylerville and Bennington to dig for relics of the Revolution. They found one belt buckle and wanted to find a smashed human bone but never did. Now everything in the collection had a number painted on it in white. The number corresponded to an entry in the large ledger that sat on the desk at the doorway of the room. The first page read: *Miniature Museum.*

If he were to keep the house, Mike thought, he could just write off the upstairs. He couldn't dispose of the collection and certainly couldn't move it. His father had always laughed at D.C.'s collection—laughs that ended in a bitter snort, as if D.C. were taking something away from him by collecting all those little things. His third year in college, Mike had written one song about the museum and another about the expeditions to the battlegrounds. If he ever made an album, he'd like a picture of the museum room on the record jacket.

For the present, his problem was that everything in the museum was dusty and fragile. He cleared away the dust on top of the closed boxes with a feather duster, but when he tried to brush off some nineteenth-century beadwork, the piece popped in his hand, and the crystal beads spelling "Roses" sprayed all over the floor. He also ruined one model plane. The old balsa was so brittle he had barely touched it when half a wing fell off. He did all right with pieces of famous rocks—Mt. Rushmore and the Blarney Stone—but he lost the silver skin of a piece of birch bark from Robert Frost's woods over in South Shaftsbury. If he kept the house, he thought, he would have to do something about the collection. If he kept the house and moved into it—if he gave up his job in New York and tried to live off savings and odd work—he could dust it every day. Perhaps he would get some songs written if he lived in the house.

His grandfather's friend Arvid Karlssen came by one evening after work. He came at around the same time D.C. used to drive in from Eagle Bridge Machine & Tool, and Arvid's Chevy looked a little like the one D.C. used to drive. But Arvid looked nothing like Mike's beanpole grandfather. Dark and squat, Arvid walked like an athlete or a sailor, like someone testing the ground. Mike offered him a beer, and Arvid accepted. He settled himself on the porch step. Mike remembered long evenings in the summer when he and Arvid and D.C. watched the sun go down, and the men talked about their lives and the factory. It seemed to Mike that those evenings were the real point of the day, the rest only a buildup to that time.

"All of D.C.'s chickens are dead," Arvid said. "The damn water froze. That boy who was supposed to come—Dan Brown, you know him?"

"Yes," said Mike, "I think I do."

"Not worth so much. Came every other day. Said it was enough for the chickens, but it wasn't when it's freezing-water time. Then something got to them. A dog, maybe. It was a terrible mess. Feathers all over."

"Did Dan clean up the place?" Mike asked. "Or did you get stuck with the job?"

"All the chickens dead. What would he clean up for? He'd done his job."

"Well. Thank you for taking care of that, Arvid. I'm sorry I wasn't here to do it myself. But done is done, I guess. I wouldn't have known what to do with the chickens in the city anyway. I only have two rooms there."

Mike expected him to smile or say, "You are a joker," as he used to, but Arvid only said, "That's twenty chickens dead." He couldn't seem to get over it, and when Mike steered the conversation to Mary, to D.C., even to their funerals, Arvid did no more than nod. Mike wondered if Arvid blamed him for the chickens or if he was really upset about D.C. and could only talk about the chickens.

"Would you like something from the collection?" Mike offered. "Would you like one of the model planes or an arrowhead?" It seemed a fair offer for the caretaking Arvid had done, but he said, "No. Wouldn't want to break up the collection. Wouldn't be right."

"I'm not sure what to do with the collection," Mike said, "to tell the truth." When Arvid didn't speak, he assumed interest and went on. "I can't throw it away, but if I keep it where it is in the house there isn't very much room left. If I wanted friends to come stay or something. And if I sell the house, what do I do with the collection? I feel like keeping the house to keep the collection. Maybe I should. They left it to me free and clear."

It was the most he'd spoken in ten days, and when there was no immediate reply from Arvid he sat back in the rocker and squinted into the sunset in imitation of the older man. Still, no reply came and no words of advice or offers of help. When a long time had passed, Arvid said "Well" several times, announced he was on his way, and stood up. The closest Mike came to getting what he wanted was when Arvid turned and waved before he started his car. Mike waited for a homily or a warning, but Arvid only said he'd see him around, started the Chevy, and drove off.

Mike went upstairs to look at the collection, wondering if he'd feel mean for describing it to Arvid as a problem. He thought that the downstairs would look better with plain white walls, that this room, cleared, would be a perfect studio, with views to the east and the south. If he lived in that house, he would have less money and more time. In the city, his ambition stalked him, but perhaps here it would give something back to him. He liked being alone in the house. His thoughts came to him in short phrases that could be sung if the right tune accompanied them. He wanted to write a song about Mary and D.C. married for fifty years, and his parents for thirty, and he couldn't imagine a weekend with a girl; about sitting on the porch waiting to hear them in the house though they were dead, and knowing any sound would be only the wind or a moth batting against a screen; about the terrarium holding the light of day, and him alone there at the round table. In New York, for every one person who wanted to sell a song there were ten who would kill to do it.

If Arvid was so worried about the chickens, he should have watered them himself. He had liked Arvid when he was a child. But the best part, he remembered, was when Arvid left and D.C. explained to Mike what he'd said that was interesting, what he meant when he spoke about the other men at the factory. Now that he looked at it, the whole memory was not so pleasant, but, Mike thought, one half couldn't exist without the other.

The second-to-last day of Mike's vacation promised to be a collector's item—a July day in May. Mike decided to do something. He could hold off selling the house; he could hold off changing the house. But in the last twelve days he'd been looking at a small shed his grandfather called the pig shed. D.C. had put it together in a day or two one summer. The shed creaked in the wind and drooped under the snow. The roof had collapsed on one side and the window was long broken. The door tilted out of jamb. Mike had proposed to D.C. two years before that they take it down. It would open up the view, he'd said, and it would be a pleasure not to look at it. It wasn't watertight and D.C. kept nothing in it; why not take it down? But D.C. hadn't wanted to. He'd stalled from day to day, and Mike had to return to the city before they got a chance to work on it. Taking down the shed was the one thing Mike was sure he wanted to do, so he got up from his rocker and approached the shed for a closer look.

The shed was built from scrap wood, full of knotholes and nail holes from former use, bleached from exposure to the weather. Half the siding was split and was parting from the supports. Mike stuck his head through the empty window frame to see if anything was inside. Mike withdrew from the building and went to the toolroom. He took out a ladder and brought it to the shed. Then he returned to the toolroom for a hammer and crowbar.

Mike set up the ladder against the sturdiest-looking wall, and climbed the ladder. He intended to take off the roofing and siding first. He started on the roof with the crowbar, but he had given D.C. too much credit. The shed, more interconnected and fragile than Mike could have seen, came apart at the first touch of the crowbar. The crossbeam collapsed, and with its loss the walls, the roof, and the rest of the supports gave way. Mike and the ladder fell forward into the pile of wood.

"I'm all right," Mike said. "I'm all right." With his free arm, he pushed some of the wood off his legs. The shed should have been in the museum, he thought. He pulled himself out of the wreckage and, a few feet away, he sat up and felt himself slowly all over. He tried moving his arms and legs. Everything worked but his left ankle. He couldn't feel any wetness or warmth from blood in his high work boots. The ankle wasn't broken, since he could move it a little from side to side.

Mike looked around at the house he owned and the lawn he'd mown so carefully. They were peaceful and indifferent to him. D.C. wasn't there to tell him what had gone wrong. Mary wasn't there to help him to the house, to take off his boot, and to bring him bowls of water to soak his ankle in. He couldn't take things apart. He couldn't put them together. He moved his foot again to test the injury, and in the pain his ankle gave him Mike looked for something definite. He wished for something to build on.

ARLENE

Summers since I graduated from college, I have shared weekend houses at the beach with friends and strangers, I've gone to the mountains to towns with names like Liberty—I've even made the run each night to Westchester, caretaking in solitude for a house whose family had abandoned it for the season. This year it was too much to think of, choosing which clothes to leave at the summer place, which to keep in the city, too much trouble to mark on the calendar which weekends were mine, which not. In much the same way I've stayed in the same job and same apartment for seven years, I decided to spend the summer in New York, to face the season on my home ground.

One Friday night in June, I fell asleep with the TV on, something I try not to do. I dislike the feeling—my dreams mingling with a Rosalind Russell movie or the Late News. I kept trying to force myself awake, to turn off the TV, get into bed, go to sleep for real. It was still early enough in summer to live without air conditioning and my windows were opened wide. Each time I woke I saw the breeze rustling the curtains, then sucking them back on to the locked security gates, making a harlequin pattern that was erased by the next exhalation of the window. Through all this sleep and waking, TV and wind, I heard a noise—a moan or a song—then distinct words, then screams. I was shocked awake as you are when you're falling asleep at the wheel. The screaming

135

stopped and the words disappeared along with my dreams. The signal pattern on the TV flickered, the curtains relaxed once more. I woke, brushed my teeth, returned to bed, and slept through the night.

I heard the same noise on several occasions, but I ignored it in favor of sleep. Summer is a slow time in publishing—whoever you want to speak with at any moment is away on vacation, though my department, Production, hums and bumps along at a routine pace. This summer there was more drama than usual. A review was so badly misquoted on the jacket of a mass-market paperback that the entire run had to be destroyed and a new jacket printed up; by the middle of July things had settled down again. I was able to come home around six, make supper, read or watch TV. Sometimes I went out again and walked around the Village until dark. Sometimes I visited with friends. The summer was unfolding itself now in dull quiet times; no rackety travel and sharing of houses but private and quiet hours at home. Even the city was shutting itself off—I noticed certain shops and restaurants shifting their hours with the sun.

My downstairs neighbor Arlene was the only other single person in the building, the only other person not leading a normal family life by neighborhood standards. This brought us together, but it was a false union. Arlene worked as a temporary and this spelled the difference between us. Arlene went from job to job, licking envelopes, typing addresses, taking shorthand as if there were no tomorrow. How she hung on to her apartment for so long I don't know. If anyone looked like a gypsy, Arlene did. We talked when we met on the stairs; sometimes we had a cup of coffee. I kept the extra set of keys to her apartment, in case she got locked out or lost her set. My extra set I entrusted to Mrs. Cassotta, who lived next to Arlene. I would have given them to Arlene, who kept more flexible hours, but I couldn't imagine where I'd find her if I needed her, or where in her apartment she would store my keys. Perhaps sensing this slight friendship, the other neighbors came to me and complained about Arlene's loud music, doors slammed at all hours, as if I were responsible, as if I could say a word and make plausible her behavior. Or better still, change it. I could change nothing, just remain a one-way street, holding Arlene's keys and listening to the others' complaints about her. Arlene's only offense against me personally was that she borrowed too much, far beyond her neighborly share of sugar and milk, flour and eggs, took enough over the years to make me an eight-layer cake, though she never did and never would.

In the midst of this summer peace—when the hot smell of urine rose from the sidewalk, when I caught a quick glance at nasturtiums in a window box, when I occasionally rose with a not yet punishing sun—Arlene threw herself out the window. Who could have predicted it? Arlene went quietly, in death as not in life. I slept through the whole thing and didn't hear her scream, if she screamed, nor the ambulance siren, nor the hoots of the police car. I had my air conditioner in by that time, no more breathing curtains, only cool air pumping into the bedroom.

The whole apartment house talked about Arlene's death. The only other deaths the house had suffered during my time were those of old grandmothers and grand-fathers, whose end was more or less expected. This death was bad; it brought the police and a bad name to the building. I tried to avoid discussing it because I didn't get a word of information from anyone, only more complaints about Arlene. Mrs. Cassotta had had to take the most from her, since their apartments were next door. Everything about Arlene from her henna hair to the noise of her rock 'n' roll grated on Mrs. Cassotta. The night after Arlene died, I came home late from work. I'd been grocery shopping and bought twice my usual supply—two full bags. Mrs. Cassotta and I met on the stairs, and she kept me there. I nodded as she recounted every exchange she and Arlene had had for years, justifying this or that piece of harshness. She held a book and a piece of lace in her hand, on her way to Mass.

"You couldn't have done anything," I said when I could get a word in. The bags of groceries were cutting into my arms, but I was reluctant to put them down, a signal that I would stay longer and listen more.

"Done anything, Marianne," said Mrs. Cassotta, and she backed away a step to show her surprise. "What could I have done? What do you expect me to do with a person like that?"

I ironed that night, an activity I connect with childhood and sadness. I grew up in New Jersey near the Delaware Water Gap, and my memories of childhood summers there are brought back by the smell of steam and cotton.

Summers were choiceless then and endless. I iron poorly and leave creases on my sleeves. I was thinking of this and that—someone to call whom I hadn't seen in a while, a record to buy over the weekend—when I remembered the suitcase Arlene had borrowed from me on a similar night the year before. Arlene was excited, for she was going out to Long Island for the weekend, not the Long Island she came from, but past the tract houses and the decent schools to Amagansett or Montauk, to protected beaches and glass cottages set on eroding cliffs. She might have been going with a group of women or with a man. Arlene needed the right size suitcase for her weekend, not too big, which would show she was insecure or inexperienced and bringing too much clothing, not so small that she would be without the right clothes. She had no real suitcase of any size, only a straw bag broken at the corners. I lent her my white canvas suitcase with the big red zipper, and I never saw it again.

Now the house was peaceful and the street quiet for once. I wanted that suitcase back, for I would get nothing else from Arlene, ever again. I didn't know why she'd killed herself, and I felt annoyed and upright. I remembered mornings dragging myself to work and as I passed Arlene's door hearing music or, worse, silence, indicating sleep and freedom. Why should she disturb the building by jumping from one of its windows into its courtyard? And why should she borrow things and never return them? I had no idea who would collect Arlene's worldly goods. All I knew was that she was from Long Island. If I'd been the one to jump, I'm sure Arlene would have had an equally hard time remembering where in New

Jersey I came from. But someone would come, and unless I did something they'd dispose of my suitcase along with the rest.

I finished the ironing and put away my clothing. I could have waited until the next day to get the suitcase but I didn't like to hurry in the morning on the way to work. Besides, if someone came during the day, I might miss my chance. I wondered who would come and where the ambulance had taken Arlene. She'd always let me know her plans, where she was going for weekends or small trips. There hadn't been much between us, but there had been that checking.

There've been two robberies in the building in the last year, so everyone listens for strange sounds in the hall. I hoped no one would discover me entering Arlene's apartment. I walked downstairs and opened her door. Her apartment is laid out exactly as mine is. I reached for the wall light switch, but the light didn't go on. Maybe Arlene had run out of bulbs and couldn't get it together to replace this one. I moved farther into the apartment toward the kitchen. I stepped on something soft but substantial, like flesh, and I reached for the light switch. The overhead light flickered on; it was a fluorescent tube, covered with specks I thought were cockroach eggs. I was standing on a bath towel. Looking from the kitchen through to the bedroom and living room, I could not distinguish between clothing and sheets piled up on chairs and piles of clothing and sheets on the floor. There were large pieces of drawing paper draped over the piles, and the papers were covered with scrawled writing. I hoped for a moment that the papers were lists, grocery lists or laundry lists. But one said BONES, over and over, another PicKs. On others random numbers—50, 17, 9— were written with different-colored Magic Markers in different sequences. A window was open and the half curtain flapped in the breeze; despite that, the apartment smelled. In the sink, dishes were piled high, and roaches scurried in the light, shocked into action.

I decided to leave the suitcase wherever it was, and I turned to go. Then I saw it by the door, sitting as if it were still waiting to go away for a weekend. Arlene had intended to return it after all. I turned off the kitchen light and walked in the dark the few paces to the door and the suitcase. There was a rustling sound from the back of the apartment. Something was moving. I saw a dark form make its way across the floor. It was Arlene's tortoiseshell cat, Hodge. "You scared me," I said. "Who's taking care of you?" The cat walked past me without looking left or right, and went out the door. Arlene had liked that cat. I'd have thought she would have given him away before she died, provided for him somehow. She was careless, I thought. I picked up the suitcase, and left the apartment as quickly as I could.

That night I slept badly, as I always do when I drink wine before I sleep. I woke once from a dream, then lay until daybreak listening to the aquatic sound of traffic moving up Sixth Avenue. Late for work in the morning, I hurried to wash and dress, and noticed the suitcase where I'd left it by my apartment door. I was sorry I'd taken it. In the light of day I regretted I'd ever wanted it back. I picked it up, intending to put it in the closet, when I noticed that the suitcase was heavier than it should have been. The night before I'd been too busy getting out of Arlene's to care. I laid the suitcase on the floor and opened it. It was filled with spiral-bound notebooks and folded drawing paper of the type I'd seen the night before at Arlene's. I opened one of the notebooks. It was a diary, and this entry dated from July two years before. Arlene was trying to find a permanent job but didn't like going to the office every day. "I hate the feeling that people are expecting me." She thought her apartment was too small and considered moving. I skimmed the rest of July looking for a mention of my name but there was none. Fair enough. The handwriting changed entry to entry: sometimes it was small and precise, sometimes a scrawl barely contained by the page. I looked at my watch, then stuffed the notebook back in the suitcase. I left the suitcase by the door and went to work.

I enjoy walking across Washington Square, even if there's rain or snow. The walk gives me time to adjust to the day ahead. This Friday morning was more like a spring day than full summer, and quite a few people failed to show up for work, taking official or unofficial three-day weekends. The only people in Production were me and Manny, one of the designers. The phone hardly rang all morning, as if a moratorium had been declared in honor of the absent. At lunchtime Manny and I got sandwiches and beer, and went up to the roof. Years ago someone had put two beach chairs on the roof and there they remained, soot-covered and warped. We settled on them— no competition for once. We talked for a while about Manny's vacation in Colorado. I started yawning deep sleepy yawns, and apologized: "I didn't sleep very well. There's been all sorts of stuff happening in my building." I told him about Arlene's suicide two nights before.

Manny was sympathetic and told me about the death of a friend that was in some ways as violent. "It's always worse for the ones who have to pick up the pieces," he said, and I told him about the suitcase and her diaries and papers. I waited for Manny to say how the city gets to people or how some people are cracked all along and need just a little tap in the right spot, but he said, "You have to get a tin box. First thing."

"Why?"

"To neutralize those papers. Once they're in your house, so's the girl. That's the way it is. Suicides don't know they're dead. They're stuck, just like they were when they died. So you can't get rid of them until they *know* they're dead. Then they can leave. This is just the first sleepless night. In my experience."

"They aren't the only ones who don't know they're dead," I said.

"I hate to come down hard on you, Marianne, but I'm telling you. You have to get a tin box and some plain white candles. You set the papers in the box, close it up so no air gets in, then put the candles one at each corner. You light them and let them burn down. When they're almost burned, you say—what's her name, anyway?"

"Arlene."

"You say—out loud—'Arlene, you're dead now. You're free now. You can go.'"

"Manny. I'd feel silly doing that."

"You want to wake up every night, that's your business. I'm talking from experience. That's not the worst thing suicides do. Wake you up. If I weren't going to the beach, I'd come over and help you."

On the way home that evening it seemed to me that the only people in New York for the weekend were me, the bums in the park, and a few seven-year-olds on skateboards. I wondered if I'd been foolish not to take shares in a place, even for every third or fourth weekend. One year Arlene took shares this late in the season, but she went out to the house only once. She said the people were too weird for her. I walked over to Sixth Avenue and then to Bleecker Street in the opposite direction from home. I bought a small loaf of bread from an Italian bakery which smelled so intensely of yeast it was a relief to be out on the street again. I lived for a year over a bakery and haven't felt the same about yeast since then. Farther down the block I stopped for a paper and spent some time looking through magazines to see if I felt like changing my image, cutting my hair, or losing weight. At the fish store I bought two small pieces of sole, crossed Sixth Avenue again, and headed home.

From a half flight below I could tell there was someone standing on the third-floor landing. The person wasn't at the door of an apartment and didn't seem to be moving. With each step, I could see a little more—whoever it was stood planted in the middle of the landing. When I got to the third floor, the figure moved into the light and I saw it was a woman. She was older than I and wore a white linen skirt and a pale blue shirt. She was dressed like a lady, and I wondered what she wanted.

"Hello." The woman's voice sounded familiar. "I wonder if you could help me," she said, more as a question to herself than to me. "I'm Arlene's sister. The girl who lived in that apartment. You knew her?"

"I knew her," I said. "Not very well."

"That doesn't matter. How well." The woman took a step closer to me. "I'm looking for her cat, so it matters more if you know her cat."

"You mean Hodge?"

"That's the name." The woman pointed to Arlene's open door. "Care to come in? Maybe I can find a tea bag or two."

"No. I don't think so. It's been a long day. How can I help you?"

"I came here looking for the cat. The Salvation Army's coming for the rest of her stuff. But Arlene wrote me a note the other week. It could have been a month for all I remember. She said if anything final happened to her, I should take care of Hodge. I thought she was kidding. She knows I hate cats."

I was about to tell Arlene's sister her troubles were over, that Hodge had left the night before and he'd looked as if he could take care of himself. But I thought I'd look shabby, going into Arlene's and taking the suitcase. Even though it was mine, it might sound like a theft of sorts.

"Are the windows open?" I asked. "Maybe he went downstairs for a walk."

"The only open window has no fire escape," she said, "and I don't think Arlene let him out of the apartment, anyway. She thought the world of him."

It occurred to me that Arlene hadn't thought very much of the world, but I suggested, "Maybe she did something with the cat. Gave him away or something and forgot to let you know about it."

The woman's face brightened. "That's a great idea. But who are her friends? I can't seem to find anyone who knew her. The funeral's going to be in Manhattan. Simple. But I can't see going around to everyone at the funeral asking for a cat." She looked more like Arlene at that moment than she had before. It was a problem Arlene might have dwelled on for days.

"I'd forget it," I said. "Leave a note downstairs by the mailboxes for someone to tell you if they see the cat."

"That's a good idea too. I guess that's all I really can do. Well. Glad I ran into you. I'll be going now," and she turned and walked into Arlene's apartment. Knowing what was inside, I admired her style. Later, as I sat before the TV news, drinking a gin and tonic, I heard a door slam on the floor below. Arlene's sister was leaving, I guessed, slamming out in just the way that annoyed Mrs. Cassotta. I looked around my apartment at the bookshelves, the built-in bed and couch; at the gates screwed into the window jambs, the curtains hung before the gated and gateless windows. They'd have to use a crowbar to remove the traces of my life from this place, but in a few more days Arlene's apartment would be cleaned and rented to someone new. Her time in this building would be forgotten. Except for the suitcase, of course, and the papers inside.

I considered returning the suitcase then, but an image of Arlene falling, her red hair streaming, came to me and I didn't think I wanted to go into her apartment again. Instead I ate a bite of fish, a hunk of bread, and thought of going to the movies. It was late to do anything. I fell asleep, still thinking I would only nap, then try for entertainment, but my sleep took me hours into the night, all the way to four in the morning. I woke hearing the words: "Bones. The bones are everywhere. I can't stand it, there are bones everywhere and the bones are no, no, no, no, no." City noises came through the open window, then a shout from below, but it was in another voice. The voice I'd woken up to had been shrill, familiar. I sat up in the dark, breathing quietly as I could, then crawled to the edge of my bed. The door was locked; the gates were closed on both the kitchen and bedroom windows, the only windows with fire escapes. I heard a sound from the living room, then recognized it as the sound of the curtain slapping against the window ledge. I looked once again at the door and saw the suitcase sitting there, waiting to embark on a voyage. Arlene had called out "Bones" before. That's what she had been saying in June, that was what I had heard through the television, the wind, and my sleep, and that was what I ignored when I heard it again, too tired to listen or to care. It was quiet after that and I slept surprisingly well, thinking that I would be minus one suitcase after all.

———

147

Saturday mornings I clean the house. Each time I passed the suitcase I gave it a look but it told me nothing. There were new problems to consider as I dusted the furniture and windowsills, as I vacuumed the floors and washed. Where would I get a tin box large enough for the suitcase and the infected papers? What would I do with the box—which would no doubt be expensive—once the ceremony was over? When the candles were burned and the words spoken to Arlene, I would still be stuck with the papers. Manny hadn't promised me they would dematerialize, only that they would be neutral. And I couldn't see telling Arlene she was dead. Arlene had always known exactly how she was. She was always announcing: "I'm so depressed, I haven't been this depressed for two weeks." Or, "I'm upset because it's raining," or because it was her birthday or Christmas or any holiday or because of a change in the weather. I'd liked her for having reasons. I go along feeling this or that but finding nowhere to pin things. I could leave the suitcase in Arlene's apartment, of course, but I wanted it out of the building.

I slipped the keys to Arlene's apartment into the suitcase and went downstairs, suitcase in hand. It was still early in the morning, before most of the shops were open. I walked along Bleecker Street, looking for the right place. I stopped and looked in the shop windows at French antiques and cotton cloth, at game birds waiting to be eaten and wheels of cheese waiting to be cut. At the end of Bleecker Street, I stopped and looked across at the playground, at the sand pits and swings, benches for the mothers. The suitcase felt heavy, tugging on my arm for attention. The only person sitting in the playground looked a good forty years too old for the place. If I left the suitcase there by a bench, he might notice and call after me, give me back the suitcase, and I'd be stuck with it again. I walked on past the playground, and turned toward the river. The block I happened to be on was one I'd considered moving to last year. It was a prettier and quieter street than mine, but the apartment was small and I'd decided against it. I tried to recall which building it had been and which apartment, and looked up into the windows, blinds down against the daylight, lace curtains drawn together and moving in the breeze from the river.

I remembered Arlene saying, "My grandfather's bones are in my legs." How could I not have listened when she said that? The row of townhouses I stood before had different-colored doors—blue, red, green, yellow. There were garbage cans in front of the blue-door house, and I walked over to them. I lifted the lid of one can and looked in. It was empty. I thought of the words Manny had told me to say, "You're dead now, you're free, you can go." I wanted to say something more personal, and I wasn't sure what it was. The curtains moved on the second floor, and I thought suddenly someone was watching me as I stood there, suitcase in one hand, lid of the garbage can in the other. I couldn't bring myself to say the words quickly or out loud, so I replaced the lid and moved away fast. I retraced my steps back up Bleecker Street, ignoring everything this time, letting the world get on without me.

———

Back in my building, I paused on the third-floor landing for breath and thought I heard the sound of the radio from Arlene's apartment. Then there was silence, the noise resumed, and I recognized that it was coming from Mrs. Cassotta's apartment.

I was relieved to get to my own apartment, to shut the door behind me, and to put down the suitcase in the place by the door where it seemed to belong. I went into the bathroom and turned on both faucets in the sink. The sound of the water was like a river at night. I could see my apartment reflected in the medicine-cabinet mirror. I saw myself reflected also, my face looking thin where I was sweating from the climb up the stairs, the cheekbones more prominent, the lines deeper around my mouth and eyes. Other summers, when I went away, a suntan brought out those lines; now they appeared on their own. I looked into the mirror beyond my own reflection, deep into the apartment, and I waited for some movement or sound that would tell me I wasn't alone. Nothing moved. Nothing spoke. I washed and dried my face and went into the living room. I stood at the window, then pushed aside the curtains, opened the window as wide as it would go, and looked down into the courtyard where Arlene had landed. I lifted my arms, letting the breeze from the courtyard coat my arms and chest. My arms felt light and I stretched them into the air as far as I could. "Arlene," I said. "What do you think I should do for the rest of the summer?" and I waited at the window for a reply, waited long enough to hear the question disappear.

NOTHING
LIKE
IT

The street wasn't much—an old-fashioned sweetshop with glass candy jars in the window, a carpet warehouse with two stories boarded up and the top story open to pigeons and climbing ivy, a butcher's with a fat yellow cat asleep across the doorway, and Little Dorrit Antiques. I'd wandered down the street from St. George's, the church where Little Dorrit was married. There was a plaque on the church saying so, just as there were plaques on buildings in Bloomsbury, where I was staying, announcing that Virginia Woolf had lived there, as though the daughter of Marshalsea and Virginia Woolf had an equal right to commemoration. The dusty window of the antique shop was crowded with goods, and the jumble continued inside—enamelled toy cars on three wheels tipping over, flowered china bowls and vases, their chips turned to the wall. Aged dolls with faded faces sagged on the shelves in unladylike postures. There were tables and chairs that looked whole at first and then could be seen to be propped up, arms and legs and wings removed or tilted at a jaunty angle. The walls were a color I couldn't name: the yellow of mustard or brewer's yeast. Shaded by a green glass cone, a single bulb shone over a large worktable. The only other light came through the dusty window, giving the shop a grainy air of resignation.

A man sat at the worktable. He wore a black turtleneck, and his hair was bright and straight. A cigarette burned at the table's edge. Lying before him was a painted wooden pony that was nearly as big as the table itself. A piece of the tail had broken off, and with a crumpled piece of sandpaper the man was patiently stroking a crescent of wood, to match the empty place. I stood at the window, waiting for him to notice me. I was wearing my brown velvet jacket, snug at the waist, and a brown velvet beret that matched the jacket and my hair. I'd pinned a tiny red grosgrain bow to the hat, and my white lace cuffs emerged from the jacket, fresh and ready. Feeling me watching him, the man looked up and smiled. He returned to his work, and I reached for the brass knob. I entered Little Dorrit Antiques as if I were an expected guest.

It was midafternoon, my seventeenth day in London. In four more days I could go home—that is, according to my airline ticket I'd be able to leave, and by the terms of my bargain with myself it would be time to go back to New York. I'd grown up there, born when my parents were old to have a baby—both of them in their forties—and the three of us lived quietly in an apartment overlooking a red stone church on Amsterdam Avenue. I'd never been farther from New York than Massachusetts, where I went to college. I don't know what I was thinking of, going there, or why I stayed. I never got used to the dark in the country or to the wind. And I was always wondering what was happening in New York, as if real life took place there exclusively.

When I came home after college, the city, instead of holding a place open for me, had closed ranks. I found myself looking for an apartment and a job like any stranger, and living in my old room off the kitchen in my parents' apartment. I woke each morning to the sound of my father setting the kettle on the stove for his morning tea, and when I heard the grains of my mother's coffee fall onto the paper filter I knew it was time to rise and join them. We sat all three at the kitchen table: my father dressed, my mother in her yellow quilted robe, and I in my flannel nightgown. Sometimes I caught them looking at one another as though they'd been played a nasty trick, their daughter returned when they should have had the place to themselves.

In the summer, through a friend of my mother's, I found a job in the circulation department of a magazine that was given away to lawyers. The magazine was full of glossy ads and glossier accounts of legal history, though the offices were gray and plain. To save money from my salary, I ate lunch at my desk every day and looked into the back windows of the hotel where the Beatles had stayed on their first visit to New York. I knew this time in my life was temporary. Something else was coming, something that would make the long days at my job worthwhile or soon forgotten.

I filled in for my mother's friend—the manager of the circulation department—when she was on vacation, and when she came back, after Labor Day, I asked if I had any time coming to me. I'd saved money for a cheap ticket to London, I told her. She'd known my mother since high school. Her own children were grown and gone. She smiled and said, "I think you do have time coming, Alice." I knew she wouldn't expect me back.

My parents were probably happy to see me go. They had always been patient with me and lavished attention on me, as if all their lives before I was born they had been saving up energy for the effort I would require. As a little girl I'd hesitated to show them small cuts and bruises for fear it would hurt them. At first, when I told them my plan they were dismayed; then they were relieved. As soon as I returned from my vacation, everything would settle in sweet as pie, my mother said. And my father gave me a crisp hundred-dollar bill in an envelope the morning I left for the airport.

At the sound of the shop door opening and closing, the man at the worktable looked up again. He was older than I'd thought, seeing him through the window. He gave me a smile that was both cordial and professional.

"Are you fond of carrousels?" he asked. He spoke as he might have sung, gently and lightly.

"I haven't been on one in years," I said. "There's a good one in Central Park."

"Ah," he said. "American."

I admitted I was American and said my name was Alice Barnstone.

"I'm Alan Boot," he said. "A horse won't be still for long, so I must press on. But have a look, Alice. Look at the dolls. Most pretty girls like dolls."

"I left mine at home," I said, but obediently I circled his store, picking up an etched glass here, a bud vase there, touching the cheek of a curly-headed Victorian baby in wrinkled petticoats. I ended by the door at a straw basket filled with buttons, medals, and buckles. I found a small metal belt buckle in the form of a woman's head, and I said, "Lovely, isn't it? I could polish it, couldn't I?" I moved closer to the table, so he could see the buckle, and I wondered if Alan Boot had chosen the color of the walls by mistake or if he'd learned to live with it.

"It looks quite like you," he said. "Though perhaps more like your older sister."

"I'm an only child," I said.

"And I've no one at all," he said in a matter-of-fact way that asked for neither sympathy nor comment. "I used to have an old auntie, but she died and left me the money to buy this place." A bell chimed, and he gestured with his sandpaper at a clock hanging above a doll's house. "Teatime already. You must be tired and thirsty."

As soon as Alan said it, I realized I was. I enjoyed walking in London, but I wasn't comfortable eating alone in public. More often than not, I bought wine, meat pies, and chocolate, and ate in my bed-and-breakfast before I went to sleep.

"Perhaps," said Alan Boot, smiling in a kind way, "you might accept a cup of tea. I have a kitchen upstairs."

At home, I'd known which blocks to walk on, which not, and never to cross the bridle path to the wild part of Central Park. It went against the grain to go upstairs with a strange man. But Alan Boot looked harmless, and the grain wasn't doing me much good. I followed him up the yellow stairwell to his parlor, where he settled me in one of two large blue armchairs that faced a modest tile mantel and an ornate iron coal grate. There was a bare modern floor-to-ceiling window behind the chairs. From the kitchen, Alan called, "See out the window? That bit of brickwork?"

"The old wall?"

"That's all that remains of Marshalsea Prison."

"Oh," I said, recognizing the name.

"Where Dickens' father was incarcerated," he explained. "Terrible for little Charles. For his father as well, I suppose, though no one seems to have any sympathy left over for him."

Alan served me one pot of tea, a plain, brown, serviceable pot, and then he switched to a white porcelain pot covered with a design of blue cornflowers—to match my eyes, he said. "You're not one of those false blue-eyed girls, are you," he asked, "with contact lenses to add to your color?"

"My eyes are true blue," I said. "Not that I had much to do with it. They came this way."

"Let me know if I'm keeping you from your evening engagement," he said.

I removed my brown velvet beret and set it on the generous arm of my chair and leaned back. He was rangy and handsome, like the men I'd seen in black-and-white movies about English working-class life. "I'm not expected anywhere," I said. "I don't know anyone in London."

I asked about his aunt—how she came to be his only

relative—and Alan told me that both his parents had been killed during the war in an air raid. "I was placed with a family near Bath," he said.

"What's it like there?" I asked, not knowing what else to say. We might go there, I thought, and quickly I imagined green fields and thatch-roofed cottages I'd seen before only on cookie tins and postcards. "Is it pretty?"

"I was no more than a year old. Didn't notice the scenery. I was sent like a lost parcel from family to family, until my auntie found me, bless her."

"And then?"

"Oh. It's all quite ordinary after that. A year or so later, my aunt sent me to school. To several schools before it was over. She was never content with my lot in life."

"But you couldn't have been more than four years old."

"More than four, surely," Alan Boot said, as if we were discussing how much tip to leave a rude waiter.

"But young, anyway," I insisted, thinking of my parents, who hadn't let me go on a crosstown bus alone until I was ten.

"That's when it's done," Alan said. "I saw my auntie on school holidays. It wasn't the worst childhood. I went to art school for a year, and when she died I bought this little house and my van."

I waited to detect a note of anger or regret or self-pity in his story, but there wasn't a trace. I'd heard people speak with more feeling about not getting into Harvard.

It had grown dark as we talked. When I stood to go, Alan stood up next to me. He was much taller than I, and slim as a sailor. His hair wasn't bright at all but a pale shade of sand. He was older than I by ten years or more, I figured—not from his story but from his eyes.

"I should be leaving now," I said, but we sat down again, and Alan took my hand. His hand was strong, and the fingers were callused at the tips.

"Will you stay?" he asked shyly, as if he'd been rehearsing the question as we sat and drank tea and talked. I wondered if he told girls like me his sad story to make them more willing to stay. "I'd like you to," he said, and I thought, Well, why not, pretending he meant I should stay for dinner.

Later, I followed him up another set of yellow stairs to his bedroom, which he'd painted bright white. The floor was bleached pine, and a peacock-blue eiderdown covered the carved wooden bed. There were no curtains on the windows, which faced the street, and no neighbors to see in—only a view of chimneys, tiled roofs, and Great Dover Street parading by.

"I don't do this sort of thing on a regular basis, you know," Alan said as we lay together on evergreen sheets.

"Do you mean making love," I asked, "or picking up customers?" I touched his bare shoulder, which was bony and pale as the cheek of a doll in his shop.

"Both," he said, and he kissed me. "It's very rare. But can't you tell?"

We parted in the morning, and I returned in the afternoon to his shop, as he'd asked me to. This time, I had to knock on the door and wait for him to come down the stairs—the shop had a "Closed" sign hanging in the window, and the door was locked.

"I've a surprise for you," Alan said when he'd kissed me and told me he liked my bright-blue shirt. "There's a place that's gone to the Americans, but it's rather nice even so—if you catch it at just the right moment."

The evening was warm, and we walked the few blocks, not holding hands but near one another, and I was glad when we touched by accident. He was leading me to the George Inn—not, he explained carefully, the kind of place he frequented with his mates but still quite a nice place. It was the last galleried inn in London, dating from the seventeenth century. The fair evening made it possible for us to sit outside in the cobbled courtyard, where coaches once pulled up. The court was shadowed by taller buildings. Pots of red geraniums and white ornamental flowers had been set out among the wooden benches and tables. I hadn't seen anything quite so English yet, and it seemed a wonderful trick that I was there with an Englishman who knew how to get our drinks and what to order.

Alan brought me a half of lager and a bag of peanuts, and for himself a pint of bitter and some crisps.

"It's a long winter ahead," he said. "Enjoy this while you can."

"Have you been in London all summer?"

"Yes," he said, "come to think of it. In days gone by, I've been known to go to France—at the least—for a few weeks' holiday. Simple, really, in the van. But I didn't have the cash to spare this summer."

"Summer must be your big season," I said, and, when

he looked puzzled, added, "In the shop, I mean. Tourists," and I tapped myself on the chest.

"Little Dorrit has no season," he said. "Just a pleasing sameness all the year round."

"Where special do you go on vacations?" I asked.

"I had my most lavish holiday a few summers ago, when I was flush. I planned to drive down through Yugoslavia in August and take the ferry across the Adriatic. But at that very moment the German factories let out, and every Turk in Europe decided to go home. And, of course, everyone from Turkey and Yugoslavia decided to see Europe—via the very same road. It was the only road, in fact. A total muddle." He paused to drink, making a disgusted face, as though there were an order to the world denied by a traffic jam.

"Bumper to bumper," he said, "and occasionally an idiot would decide he was fed up and he'd try to pass."

"Oh dear," I said. I wondered if he was alone on his holiday, imagining him younger and accompanied by a blond English girlfriend, a Diana or Fiona, to whom he joked in his easy way as they inched along.

"Precisely," he said. "Head-on smash with the opposite traffic, just as thick."

"But couldn't you do something?" I asked. "Couldn't anyone? If there was an accident?"

Alan looked puzzled, as though I'd missed the whole point. "One couldn't get through to pick up the bodies," he said slowly, almost angrily. "Much less in time to save anyone."

I couldn't see the point of telling me such a story, and I felt like a child who'd asked a question that betrayed a lack of comprehension. It was closing time, and we had another round. This time, he had a shot of whiskey with his beer—to guarantee sweet dreams, he said.

On the way back to the shop, we came to Little Dorrit's church. We walked up the steps and read the inscription on the plaque.

"You know," I said. "This is why I found your street."

"Good for you," he said, taking my hand and kissing it. "Many profess to love Little Dorrit, but few find her."

I felt as proud as when my father had praised an awkward drawing or a stiff little book report. Alan's was the same tone as my father's, one of surprise and pleasure, as though a flower had recited the Bill of Rights. While we walked along the narrow street, I wondered if Alan had been happy in the past with another lover—an Englishwoman, who understood when to laugh at his jokes and what to take seriously. Alan unlocked the door to the shop, and when we were inside he put his arms around me and said, "Am I all right for you? Really all right?"

"Of course," I said, and I smiled at him, for his question and for relief that he wasn't bored with me already. "You're just the best thing that's happened to me ever."

In his sleep that night Alan was restless, turning from side to side. He said a word—"night," "delight"—I couldn't quite hear. I wished I'd been there with him in Yugoslavia. I would have done something. I thought of returning home in a few days, and while it seemed inevitable it also seemed as though my time in London were just beginning. I tried to imagine myself in less than a week, walking along Broadway, then saw myself, instead, with Alan on the steps of Little Dorrit's church. There must have been something to do, I thought, there's always something—and then I, too, slept.

The next morning, I moved from the bed-and-breakfast to Alan's. Without much talk about the future or each other, we drove from the square in Bloomsbury where I'd been staying back to Southwark and Little Dorrit, and he carried my suitcase upstairs to the bedroom. I hung my brown velvet jacket in his closet and put the rest of my clothing in a drawer he'd emptied for me.

"There," he said. "Just like home, and better than a hotel."

While he stood at the bedroom door, watching, I took my airline ticket and passport from my purse and set them on the dresser with Alan's collection of pennies and stray teapot lids.

"The ticket," I said. "It's good for forty-five days."

"Well," Alan said, smiling and moving his hand along the doorjamb, "that's an extended holiday, isn't it? A good, long time to see London."

But come the forty-fifth day, I meant to tell him, I still could stay. I bent over the drawer, pretending to refold my rumpled cotton shirts. I put the empty suitcase under the bed and turned around to face Alan. He would say something now, I thought, something to reassure me that I could stay as long as I liked.

"Well," he said.

"A well's a hole in the ground," I said.

We stood looking at each other, until Alan smiled and came across the room. For a moment, I was going to ask him if he really thought it was a good idea for me to be there, but when he kissed me I was glad I'd stayed silent.

That afternoon, I wrote my mother's friend and told her I wouldn't be coming back to the circulation department. Then I composed a letter to my parents, explaining that I'd stumbled on this very nice place. I described the shop and Alan in the most cheerful terms, urging them to read *Little Dorrit*. I wrote the letters from the shop, having cleared a space on one of the sturdier tables, and as I thought up phrases with which to explain that I wasn't coming home just yet, I considered the changes I'd make in the shop, the irresistible order I'd bring to it.

"Little Dorrit certainly had a terrible time," I wrote, "but in the end she managed to carve out her own kind of cozy happiness. I'm hardly Little Dorrit—lucky me!— but maybe there's some coziness waiting around here for me. We'll see," I ended temperately.

From the start, I envied the smooth grooves Alan glided in, the habits he'd built up over the years. At eleven, he'd walk across Borough High Street and buy a sweet roll for himself and one for me. Then he'd work in the shop until lunchtime. Most afternoons, he disappeared to one pub or another, where he met his pals, played darts, gossiped about antiques, and made deals. I went along once or twice, but soon quit the practice. I was terrible at darts and I could tell I was cramping the conversation. In the evening, Alan would reappear and take me to the movies or we'd cook dinner. On Sundays, there were the papers and a visit to a museum or a friend.

By way of doing my share, I kept the shop open while Alan went off in the afternoon. The first days, I sat reading a book, waiting for customers. Then I set myself the task of washing the shopwindow. This took the whole of my first week. Before cleaning the window on the inside, I had to clear my way to it. In the deep display shelf were fire engines and tea sets, all covered with dust, beaded bags, and one doeskin glove embroidered with edelweiss. Because I was careful not to break anything, it took the whole of one afternoon to clear away even half the display. When Alan came home and saw what I was doing, he raised an eyebrow and praised my ambition. But he soon suggested we go out for a drink and told me to wash my face. For the next few days, he made no comment at all, and sidestepped the goods as he entered and left. By the end of the week, the window was clean and the window display restored, free of dust and much better for the handling it received. The yellow walls still made the shop too dark, but that could be changed.

"Sweet," Alan said when I called his attention to the finished product.

"Don't you think more customers will come in now?" I asked. "Now that you can see it? That first day, I couldn't have seen you if you hadn't been sitting under the light."

"Who is there to look in on us?"

"I don't know. Tourists from the George, if they knew it was here. They'd come."

"You'd like it to be Kensington Market, I can see. Customers and dealers trampling one another up and down the aisles."

"There isn't any room here for anyone to trample," I said. "Maybe I can clear a few paths."

"This is mercantile fervor indeed," he said, and he took me to an Indian place for curry, to clear my head.

I soon learned that few customers entered Little Dorrit—only friends of Alan's come for a visit or a trinket, or people from the neighborhood who wandered in and soon backed out when they saw their mistake. "There was a greengrocer here before the war," Alan said, "and the poor dears still come of an afternoon, hoping for their bit of veg." The adventurous ones paused by the basket of buttons and medals near the door. I had observed more than one customer dip a hand in the basket, come up with something familiar, and go through a dance of recognition, remembrance, and final rejection.

"It's a waste of your time," Alan said when he came downstairs at noon one day and found me with the dolls in one corner of the shop as I tried to decide where to place them to best advantage. "Things will only move around again and be all jumbled up. The window will be filthy in no time. Why bother? Read a book. Paint your nails. Take up smoking."

"But, Alan. Things could always change."

"Ah, youth," he said, easy and smiling. "You're sweet to think it, but things are all right as they are."

"You told me yourself how once you wanted this to be the place in London people brought things for repair. And you'd be the master repairer."

"And once I wanted to join the circus. Will you have a morning bun with raisins or one stuffed with jelly?"

The truth was, Alan made his living not from sales but from cosmetic repairs to dubious pieces of furniture he bought for a song and resold to other dealers. Sometimes when I watched him work, he seemed completely happy. "It's amazing what life French polish can bring to an old piece," he'd say. Because he owned a van, his friends let him in on a moving deal now and again. "I get by," he'd say, "with a little change in my pocket, and that's all I ask."

One evening in late September, when it was almost dark, Alan arrived carrying loose in his arms a bundle of Victorian clothing and linen he'd bought that day at auction. As he came in, he stumbled over a box that I'd meant to move out of the way.

"What's all this?" he asked. "Clear a place, won't you, on that table."

"It's white paint," I said. "Dianthus White—for the shop and the stairwells. It's not really a harsh white at all, more like a white that's tempered. With a little red in it, but not much red. And it isn't pink at all. It's beautiful, Alan, I promise. The shop on Borough High Street delivered it for free."

I couldn't tell from his expression what he thought, but he dropped the bundle on the table and said, "Darling, this isn't a garden. Dianthus White, indeed—when you've about a pound left to your name. Why spend it on my old walls?"

"The place would look so wonderful. Think how nice the white bedroom looks," I said.

"The walls were painted years ago with good-quality oil paint, and they'll last the century. I'll ring the shop in the morning and they'll come for the paint. It's too sweet of you. Now, help me here if you want to help."

"But, Alan—"

"If I wanted the walls white, I'd paint them. You don't think I'm incapable, do you?"

Together we were sorting through the clothing and linen, separating the unmendable from the possible, when Alan held up an embroidered blue velvet vest and said, "Perfect for you. Big blue eyes and dark ringlets. Souvenir of Victorian London." When I put the vest on, it fit. He made me stand up, and he walked all around me, pulling my shirtsleeves through and arranging my shirt collar flat on top of the curlicues of yellow, white, and red flowers. He turned me around to see the vest from all sides, and said, "It was made for you. Anyone could see that."

I took off the vest and laid it on the pile of possible sales. "You'd best iron it and sell it," I said. "Little Dorrit's cash flow."

"I knew you were feeling low," Alan said. "I thought I caught you looking pensive when I came in. You mustn't expect so much, Alice. People just live. Day to day. That's all we're doing, you and I."

"But surely there's more than that," I said.

"Don't try so hard," he said, as though I had a nasty habit I could be cured of with encouragement. "It's a bit of a waste of energy, isn't it?"

I was afraid that if I pressed the point he might say, "Well, if this doesn't suit you, hadn't you best seek greener pastures? Life's for the living, after all."

Seeing my face, Alan came over to where I stood by the table. He held me for a few minutes, patting me on the back as if I'd been crying. "I am fond of you," he said.

"What's fond?" I asked.

"I'm awfully fond of you," he repeated. "That's all it means." For a second, he looked uncomfortable, then said, "Very fond."

For days after, I wondered what it really meant and if it was the same as an American saying, I love you. I put the dolls back where they'd been and stayed in the shop quietly. Ahead I saw the long intermission of winter, of days alone in the shop and nights with Alan. One afternoon when Alan came back from the pub, I took a walk alone, and when I returned the box of paint was gone. The money I'd paid for the paint was lying on Alan's dresser upstairs, along with my passport and ticket.

Sometimes, walking home from the pub with Alan at night, it was dark as the country and it seemed we were very lucky, the only people awake in all of Southwark. I pretended we'd been together for years and would stay together always. But even at those moments I felt as if a chore had been left undone or a promise unkept. Or worse, as if there were some simple trick I might perform, something I hadn't yet thought of, that would make everything all right.

———

One Saturday, I woke before Alan and went downstairs to heat water for tea. I sat in an armchair in the parlor and looked through the newspaper Alan had brought the night before. He rolled his papers, tucked them under his arm, brought them home, and forgot about them. I stacked them like logs in a corner of the shop.

The parlor needed dusting and the ashtrays were full. The mystery I was reading lay on the floor, and two pairs of shoes were scattered from the night before. I looked on the mantelpiece for my keys and wallet, took the spare change that lay there, and went out as quietly as I could, leaving the shop sign on "Closed." I thought of leaving a note for Alan, but I didn't know where I was going or how long I'd be gone. For a block, I worried that he would worry, and then I stepped along.

I walked toward the river, passing small plain houses where children sprawled out on the streets and women stood holding bundles and talking in the sun. For a moment, I envied them all. They were embedded in their lives and, if not content, set in place.

I walked on, across the bridge to the City, on and up to the part of London I hadn't been in much since the day I moved to Alan's. I ambled as slowly through the City as if I were still in the dark shop thinking of walking. When a passerby touched me by accident, I was shocked to be reminded I was really there. I might have disappeared that afternoon. I might have gone on walking to another neighborhood, stood before another window, entered another shop. I might have said, "Hello, I'm Susan," or Fiona or Diana, and I might have started something else. As I walked, I thought of New York, and, keeping my eyes strictly on the sidewalk, I might have been there.

I came to the American Express office near Pall Mall and went inside. In my pocket I had the hundred-dollar bill my father had given me, and my ticket. I stood in line and listened to the familiar voices, identifying the harsh vowels of the Midwest and a soft drawl, like a cowboy's from the movies. I could be home, I thought, in a few hours—a possibility that hadn't occurred to me before. I was breathless for a moment; then it was my turn, and I exchanged my dollars for pounds. Holding the fresh money in one hand, I looked around the crowded room. There was a knot of people, searching for the lines for currency, tickets, reservations, all talking, it seemed, and high above their heads were travel posters, of Greece and France, of San Francisco. I found the line for reservations, one hand holding the crisp paper money, the other stroking the airplane ticket in my pocket.

Much later, I walked south again, toward the river, and as I walked I tried to see very clearly what was around me—black taxis, bicyclists, shopwindows filled with pocketbooks and umbrellas, handkerchiefs and undershirts, the sky a pale blue at the end of a limp day. When I was tired of walking and of trying to see, I got on a bus. I chose an empty seat near the back. With no one sitting near me or beside me, I watched through the window as if I could record and hold every passing scene framed by the double-hung window of the red double-decker bus. We rolled down a hill and onto Waterloo Bridge. It was getting on toward evening and the light was dwindling. At the middle of the bridge, the bus stopped. There didn't seem to be any reason why it had stopped—I heard no honking horns from a traffic jam, nor had the engine stalled. In the silence the engine chugged like the heart of a heavy beast. I looked across the wide river and saw that a pink halo had formed around the Festival Hall. I felt suspended as surely as if I were in midair, a part of the light behind the great buildings on either bank, a part of the moving water beneath. I knew then why Alan had told me about his traffic jam in Yugoslavia. He'd been frightened when he saw he was unable to turn around, to speed up or slow down. I touched my ticket and the slip of paper on which the time of my flight was written. I felt completely happy and then the bus lurched forward and crossed the river.

In front of St. George's, Little Dorrit's church, I got out. The columns were so thick and the white-faced clock in the tower so solid and final. Borough High Street had emptied for the night, and for once looked orderly and dignified, down to the plants visible through an uncurtained window and the yellow cat that lay sleeping in the butcher's doorway.

It was quiet when I walked into the shop. The door was wide open, though the sign said "Closed." I shut the door against the cool evening air, and from habit I checked the cashbox before going upstairs. In the parlor, the fat blue armchairs glowed in the failing light, and I smelled an odor that was neither sharp nor sweet. I went up the next flight of stairs, and on the third-floor landing I nearly tripped over Alan Boot.

He was sitting on the bleached-wood floor of the bedroom doorway, smoking a cigarette, his back resting against the open bedroom door. I saw shadows for his cheeks and darkness where his eyes were. When he looked up and smiled at me, I caught a flash of whiteness—teeth, eyes—and the outline of his soft straight hair.

"Hello," he said sleepily, in his musical voice. "You've been gone a long time."

"It's almost dark," I said. "Why are you sitting here?"

"Thinking," he said. "Contemplating my work. Where have you been?"

"I went over the river," I said, "and I walked around for a while near Leicester Square. I don't know. The time just went. One thing and another. Then I took the bus home. And you?"

I turned away from Alan and looked where he was facing. I recognized the smell then—it was fresh paint. The far wall of the stairwell was a different color now, painted top to bottom. It wasn't the white I'd chosen— nothing like it. The wall was maroon, the theatrically blood-dark shade of a summer sky at sunset, wonderfully deep. It was a color I would never have considered and I couldn't have guessed that Alan would either, not if I stayed with him for a million years.

"I'm leaving," I said. "I went to American Express and made a reservation. Only three days more of me."

"Are you?" he replied. "Yes. It must be nearly time for your ticket to expire. Well. It won't be the same without you, will it? All on my own." I looked at Alan to see if he was sorry, but his face was more masklike than before and the glow of his cigarette cast light only on his smooth, full lips.

He'd known all along, then, that I'd go, that I'd keep faith with my ticket. He must have been waiting politely, hoping I'd leave sooner, leave his shop and his orphan life, pack quietly and depart without a fuss, spare him the trouble even of a sad parting. And when I was gone and Alan was alone with Little Dorrit, he'd hug himself to himself, and vow to be more careful next time and find someone who promised even less trouble than I.

"That color makes a real difference," I said.

"It took me hours to find the right shade. And it wasn't easy painting that high up, tiptoe on top of chairs and such. My side's aching."

"I can imagine," I said.

"You don't think it's too dark, do you?" Alan asked. "That was the subject of much inner turmoil."

"Too dark? It may be a shade too dark at this time of day," I said, "but in the morning it'll be something else—you'll see." I squinted my eyes, blurring everything together—Alan, myself, the stairwell as it had been and the way it was now.

FOR
SCALE

I was moving far away, leaving the East for the first time. My sister and I arranged to meet at the Port Authority to take an evening bus to the Berkshires, to visit our parents at their summer house. We would stay one night.

At the bus station, I looked in Whelan's for postcards of New York, and I thought of the people I was leaving. I would send them cards from my stops on the long drive South. I saw my sister at another postcard rack, one aisle down from mine. She was turning the rack discontentedly, as if she wanted a view of Manhattan they hadn't taken. I watched her for a few minutes, waiting for her to notice me, but I'd ordered a coffee to go and gotten it from the counterman before she looked up from the cards.

We rode through a sultry Indian-summer evening, leaving the Hudson, leaving the Bronx River, until we reached the green places, the one where I'd gone to camp, the towns in Connecticut and Massachusetts too small for a post office, gone in a wink. The green became deeper as we rode, and by the time we arrived in Great Barrington it was nearly dark. I could just make out my father standing across the street at Melvin's Pharmacy, where he'd told us the bus would let us out. He was waiting for us to see him, waving to be sure we knew where we were. He waited for the light to change and came

179

across the street to help us with our bags. The town looked black and green to me, so quiet after the city.

On the drive to the house, I could barely make out the woods. The house is shaped like a cuckoo clock; the light coming through the windows made it look inviting. The lawn felt cool as we walked the small incline to the front door. My stepmother had lit a fire for us in the stone fireplace and held two portions of supper. My sister and I were seated next to each other so we both faced the fire as we ate. My sister left the table twice to be sure her oboe was warm enough in the bedroom where she'd left it. She keeps the oboe wrapped in a Mylar blanket in its case, but still she worries that it will crack when there are changes in the temperature. We went to sleep right after dinner, and it was a deep sleep for me, one minute into darkness.

In the morning, my sister and I woke at the same time. We were sleeping in the back room, the one most sheltered, and it was impossible to tell if it was early or late. The house is set in the woods under ancient pines that steal the sun. The curtains were drawn, and the panelling gave off a slight smell of pine. My parents bought the house when I was in college, and I hadn't spent many nights there. I thought about packing up my own place—what I should take, what I would leave.

My stepmother had eaten hours before and wasn't in the house, so my father made eggs and English muffins for the three of us, and served them on the screened-in porch. He talked about the trip to Europe he and my stepmother had made last spring.

"We thought we'd play it by ear," he said, "not make

any reservations, but we didn't count on several obstacles—one of which was Easter. Everyone told us, 'Oh, we can't help you now, we're getting ready for Easter,' and after Easter it was just the same."

But eventually they reached the navel of the universe—Delphi—and travelled to Crete, visited Minoan ruins, loved the Cretan people, drove on switchback roads to the high hidden villages.

Why is it so difficult for me to listen to other people's tales of travel? Am I jealous of their good times without me or are the stories badly told? Rather than listen, I watched my father and thought what a good picture it made—him in his plaid shirt and golf cap against the background of screen and pines.

The talk went from Greece to Latin, a language all three of us had studied with varying degrees of success. My father was the best of us. I never understood as he helped me struggle with Caesar and Cicero how he could remember anything when he'd been out of school so long. My sister had one year of Latin, all in tutorial, but never got past Caesar. Soon my father and I were remembering lines from Vergil:

Forsan et haec olim meminisse juvabit.

"The ship is sinking," my father said, "and sea monsters are rising up to meet the crew. All seems lost. And Aeneas says, 'One day we'll look back even on this and smile.' "

I couldn't remember where my lines came from, but I remembered what they meant:

En Priamus. Sunt hic etiam sua praemia laudi;
Sunt lacrimae rerum et mentem mortalia tangunt.

"Ah, Priam," Aeneas says. "Even here there's praise for you, and human tears for human things, and mortals being held in mortal memory."

After we cleaned up the breakfast dishes, my sister and I went outside. We walked around the house, surveying the lawn our parents had smoothed and extended, the woods they'd thinned, the paths they'd carved for walks. Then we found our stepmother on the new patio out front. She was sitting in a lawn chair, listening on her portable radio to the House Assassinations Committee. She'd been listening to it all month, she said. My sister and I pulled up aluminum lawn chairs and formed a half circle with her, our faces up to the sun that trickled through the trees. I remembered coming home from school at lunchtime during a certain spring of my childhood to find my mother listening to the HUAC hearings then being broadcast. Years later, when I saw a famous documentary on HUAC and Joe McCarthy, I misunderstood what I saw, and thought it must be a continuation of the lunchtime show my mother had liked.

My father appeared with his camera and started circling us to get the photos he wanted—of me and my sister, then my sister and stepmother, then the three of us together. He asked us to turn our heads, then to look as if we were talking to one another. When my sister protested having her picture taken, he said what he really

wanted was a picture of the house and the pots of tomatoes and flowers on the stone steps. We were only serv-
ing as figures in the foreground, for scale.

Enough. After a few more pictures, my sister and stepmother had had enough. My stepmother turned off the
radio and we all walked into the woods to see the new gazebo.

The gazebo sits on a cliff deep in the woods overlooking a rushing brook—a good spot for trout, my father
says. The previous winter, vandals had destroyed the
original gazebo, and now, after the insurance claims had
been made and my stepmother had been diligent in looking for bargains in gazebos, there was this new screened-
in structure, bigger and sturdier, better in every way.
The roof was yellow and white, like a circus tent. We admired it from the outside, then went in. The furniture
was new also, redwood and chrome with yellow cushions.
The chairs had been delivered ready to assemble, my
stepmother said, with some necessary nuts and bolts left
out; she'd made three extra trips to Pittsfield to collect
the missing parts.

My father took one more photo; then I asked for the
camera to take a picture just of my parents. I stood as far
back as I could in the gazebo, and my father told me to
stop fooling around with his camera. "It's focussed," he
said. "I focussed it for you." But I had to bring together
the double image between my parents of the pine trees
and the screen, and a little bit of my father's shoulder.
After that, I handed the camera back to my father.

"How many shots are left on that roll?" my stepmother asked, and my father said there was only one.

"Then take a picture of the sound of the brook," she said.

My father said he would use the last shot for a study of the woods, and he went to the door of the gazebo. I told him I guessed he would really take a last picture of the three of us sitting on the new furniture.

"No," he said. "You can't get a picture through the screens."

I could tell that my sister was getting restless, that she was ready to move on to friends with whom we were visiting for the rest of the weekend. I didn't mind any of it—the gazebo, the woods, the photographs. I wanted copies of every one of them. After all, I was going so far away.